Uncle Chris's *Second* Collection of Crafty Short Stories

By P. Frost

Published by New Generation Publishing in 2024

Copyright © P. Frost 2024

First Edition

The author asserts the moral right under the Copyright, Designs and Patents Act 1988 to be identified as the author of this work.

All Rights reserved. No part of this publication may be reproduced, stored in a retrieval system or transmitted, in any form or by any means without the prior consent of the author, nor be otherwise circulated in any form of binding or cover other than that which it is published and without a similar condition being imposed on the subsequent purchaser.

ISBN 978-1-83563-564-3

www.newgeneration-publishing.com

New Generation Publishing

Confidential

The twist-meister is back!

Welcome to *Uncle Chris's **Second** Collection of Crafty Short Stories*.
This is the second book in the short story series by *Uncle Chris*.

The first book in the series, *Uncle Chris's Collection of Crafty Short Stories*, is available from all bookshops and also as an eBook.

"It's not what you do that catches you out, it's usually what you don't do!"

Professor Retep Tsorf

To Ben and Rosie

Maybe you'll read this one!

Preface

The winter of 1985 was a particularly bitter one, especially up in the hills of North Wales. It was another very cold, dark winter's night high up in the snowy Welsh mountains. Uncle Chris, now an old man, sat in front of his roaring log fire and was enjoying the many delights of his secluded luxury log cabin, which was situated next to a lonely tarn, halfway up one of the highest and coldest mountains in Wales.

Uncle Chris's favourite moment was sitting in his expansive leather armchair in front of the evening log fire, with lit candles all around the floor providing the only light for the large room. This gave him the ambience he wanted to read his twisty stories to his favourite guests.

With him in his log cabin was Sandy, his granddaughter. He might be a grandad, but everyone called him Uncle Chris, especially his family. Now, since the war a retired Physiotherapist and amateur sleuth, Uncle Chris could spend a little of his retirement time with her and this weekend it was to be a few days for them together in the cosy secluded chalet. Sandy was a fit and athletic youngster, a relief for Uncle Chris as so many offspring nowadays waste away sitting unhealthily in front of a computer. She was clever, outgoing and loved listening to evening stories from Uncle Chris while sitting in the dim light of the roaring chalet fire.

Sandy now sat opposite Uncle Chris in a comfy chair with just the glow of the fire and the candles to enable her to see. She knew about his cunningly created stories and never managed to work out the twist at the end. He had crafted them carefully and tested them on Jade, his gorgeous wife. She had a sharp-witted brain and had finetuned the stories, so now they were ready to spring on Sandy. A while ago Uncle Chris compiled the stories in a book and was now ready to read them out to her in the glow of the fireside. She had to work out what the ending would be before he himself got to the end of the story. She was always fooled.

Uncle Chris had written fifteen stories for this book. He had time tonight for three stories to read to Sandy before bedtime. It would be the last three stories in this book that he would read to her, but do read the first few beforehand..........

Uncle Chris's *Second* Collection of Crafty Short Stories

Short Story	Title
1	Doing a Favour
2	The Guardian Angel
3	The Glass Makers Delight
4	Show Me Yours and I'll Show You Mine
5	The Kayak
6	The Scam
7	The Savvy Barmaid
8	The Coach Ride
9	Keep It Close to You
10	A Dodgy Day in London
11	Vices and Desires
12	The Key To A Good Jury
13	The Perfect Escape
14	To Do or Not To Do
15	Life's a Breeze

Short Story 1: Doing a Favour

Doing a favour for someone is of course great, but it can get you into some unusual situations. For Christoph, it meant that he was about to have an enlightening experience.

Christoph is a very proud young man. He is not just a blood donor but is called upon every other month to donate a pint of blood to a specific patient, who matches his blood type. Christoph has a rare blood type and a plasma matrix that the hospital has told him matches perfectly a particular patient who is very ill, so Christoph gets a regular call to save the life of this unknown individual. It makes him feel good about himself. Christoph is happy to help but confidentiality means that the hospital cannot let him know who the patient is. Christoph doesn't realise it but he is soon to find out who the patient is.

Christoph did quite well for himself after leaving school. He got a job in his home village of Eghampton in Devon at the local newsagents, which is run by Mrs Watmore and her son. She is a lovely lady who is well known in the village for running the shop and also for her charity work. She always makes the huge shop window look appealing to potential customers, with either some flowers or a huge soft toy to entice people to look in the shop. The soft toy is then raffled off for charity. Today there is a ginormous cuddly bear in the shop window.

Mrs Watmore pays Christoph well, and as he still lives with his parents his new job leaves him flush with a little money every month. As if that wasn't enough, he has now found himself a new girlfriend. Jade moved into a flat in Christoph's village a while ago, having started a new job at the village solicitors. Christoph thinks that Jade has a gorgeous personality, is good looking and is also great fun to be with. They met in the local pub and have now been seeing each other for a couple of weeks. Both seem happy with how things are progressing. They share the same interests, laugh at similar things, and both are football mad, supporting their local football club, Plymouth Argyll. Both are pleased that they beat Brentford last week.

Christoph is so focused on his new job that he forgets about being a blood donor for a while, and when he gets the call to come urgently tomorrow it comes as a surprise. Of course he will help, he tells the hospital. The hospital is only two stops on the train, so it's very easy to get to. Christoph is particularly looking forward to the visit this time as his Gran is also in the hospital at the moment after a fall at her home, so he plans to see his Gran after he has donated blood.

On the morning of the visit to the hospital Jade tells him that she will also be going to Plymouth that morning to do some shopping. Her friend Diana will take her she adds quickly, suspiciously quickly thinks Christoph as he was hoping they could travel there together on the train. Her manner is strange so Christoph suggests meeting up afterwards, but Jade declines. Christoph is disappointed at the decline, but perhaps he is being too demanding and it might be that she just wants a girlie day out with Diana, he hopes.

On the train to the hospital he sits opposite a man wearing a Plymouth Argyll football scarf who says he is looking forward to the game. Next to him is a bald-headed girl who looks very pale and says to him that she is also going to the hospital. Christoph asks why, then realises that asking this is a little rude, especially as the girl shies away from replying. She then changes the subject. The conversation makes him wonder who else on the train is going to the hospital. The train is very convenient for the hospital so there may well be a few who are going there and, who knows, perhaps one of them is the patient needing his blood? However, that could be anyone in the county, or even the country.

Christoph gets off the train and knows that next door to the hospital there is a shop that sells flowers. Being next to the hospital, the flower shop does a good trade, and Christoph supports them by buying some for his Gran. He sees a strange, but eye-catching bunch of ten white tulips with a single red tulip in the middle, wrapped in blue cellophane. Christoph has never seen white and red tulips like that together. That should cheer Gran up he thinks.

Once in the hospital Christoph gets a pleasant surprise. His Gran is no longer there as she was discharged earlier in the day. That means she is fit and well. However, he now doesn't know what to do with the flowers. He has no one to give them to, so he looks at the nurse who will take his blood and asks if she can give it to the unknown patient who will receive his blood. The nurse smiles and says she has never seen ten white tulips together with a single red tulip in the middle, and they look great, so she will pass the flowers on to her. Christoph smiles to himself because the nurse said the word "her." So, whoever is getting his blood is female. He also later hears the nurse tell the doctor that that this person lives nearby. Christoph wonders if perhaps he has seen this person today without realising. He feels like Sherlock Holmes now.

After his blood is taken he goes to the canteen and has a sugary coffee and cake to recover. The café is full and he sits opposite a tired looking middle-aged blond lady and they have a pleasant but quick chat. Christoph wonders why she is in the hospital.

Once he has finished eating he gets up to leave and when he gets to the toilet, he notices that someone is sitting in the seat he has just vacated and he realises that it is the bald-headed girl that he saw on the train. Christoph hopes that she is okay, as she still looks as pale now as she was when they were on the train.

Then, there is a huge shock for Christoph as he sees his girlfriend Jade at a distance, at the other end of the hospital hallway. She meets his gaze, looks away quickly and walks off. He wanders why she is here. She didn't mention going to the hospital. No wander she didn't want to meet up if she was coming to the hospital as well. They have only been seeing each other for a couple of weeks so he can't expect her to tell him that she is coming here, of all places. It might be personal and it might explain why she was so guarded earlier.

He gets back on the return train for home with lots of thoughts in his mind. The train gets to his stop and as he gets off the train he sees the bald-headed girl again. This isn't a surprise as this is the last train back home so she wouldn't have wanted to miss it. He apologises for saying the wrong thing earlier. The girl smiles and tells him that it's okay. She is happy now as the hospital has now fixed her hearing aid, so all is well. She is still looking pale though.

Christoph walks back home to his parent's house. He rings Jade, his girlfriend, as he wants to know if she is okay and wonders why she had to be at the hospital. However, Jade doesn't pick up the call or even return the call, and also doesn't reply to his texts later that evening. Christoph has a restless nights sleep that evening.

The next morning Christoph has breakfast at home and gets ready for work at the newsagents. After breakfast he looks at his phone. There is still no text from Jade and he is now getting worried. Is she ill? Does she want to split up with him?

He leaves the house and walks to work. When he arrives at the shop he greets Mrs Watmore in the shop and gets ready behind the counter. Then, there is a buzz from his pocket where his phone is. He fears the worst as he sees that he has a new text, and it is from Jade.

She is texting him to say that she is sorry for not telling him about the hospital visit, but her cortisone injection for her neck pain went well, and she is now pain free which means she can join the rowing club again and restart her training at Eghampton sports centre. She even suggests a drink in the local pub tonight. The sensitive Christoph is happy now that Jade still wants to be with him. They are back in love again.

Christoph smiles to himself and starts to get the shop ready for the day.

He then looks to his left and in the huge newsagent shop window, the enormous cuddly bear has been taken away by Mrs Watmore. She has replaced it with a bunch of ten white tulips, with a single red tulip in the middle, wrapped in blue cellophane.

Mrs Watmore could only have got this set of red and white flowers from the nurse at the hospital after Christoph had passed them on to her. So that means Mrs Watmore....

Christoph looks at Mrs Watmore with his mouth gaping open. She is receiving his blood to keep her alive.

He now knows that it is her, but she doesn't know that it is him.

Short Story 2: The Guardian Angel

There has been much anxiety in the city of Hull over the last six months. Six young girls, all with long blond hair, have been strangled to death by a serial killer after leaving the pub to go home. Not only is the killer still at large, but he is on the lookout tonight for another blond girl.

All the attacks have taken place when each of the young girls have left a pub on a dark, cold night when visibility is poor. The serial killer who has committed the crimes has been labelled the Dark Stalker by the papers, as he has committed the crimes at night and is targeting girls.

The Dark Stalker has not left any clues. Even the police are unsure as to his identity, but they do state that he is very dangerous and he has a similar profile to that of the Yorkshire Ripper of the 1970's. The police did think they had caught the villain a while ago but while their suspect was behind bars a sixth murder took place, so they were holding the wrong man and the serial killer was still at large. They have told the papers that they now think the killer has recently moved to Hull from further north. All the young girls in and around Hull have been asked to be careful when returning home from an evening out during the long, dark winter evenings.

The local community have taken some action now to help vulnerable girls. Recently, a set of local young community spirited men formed a group called the Hull Guardian Angels. Each approved member of the group would visit venues such as pubs and nightclubs then keep an eye on any potential vulnerable female occupants of these establishments during the evenings. If they see a girl who may be at risk then they will discreetly follow her so that she gets safely home. Other countries have tried this strategy with some success and it has worked particularly well in America.

Tonight, Sue is sitting at the bar in The Bell which is her local pub. She is a tall blond girl full of confidence and is a person who likes to think that she can look after herself. The pub is usually full of youngsters having a good time, but tonight is a Monday night so it is not full and the modest crowd are quietly enjoying a drink. The mood is low as everyone has heard about the latest murder. The people in the pub don't know that the Dark Stalker is about to strike tonight.

Jack is the owner of The Bell. He is a bearded, middle aged man who recently moved to Hull from Glasgow. He has run the pub for years and knows most of the people who come to drink there. He is a sucker for pretty girls so it was no surprise that the charming Molly was offered the job as barmaid soon after he arrived. Between the two of them they keep the pub running. Jack quietly gets on with providing food and drink to all who visit and tends to keep himself to himself. It is not busy tonight in the pub so he spends his time tidying up and keeping a beady eye on everyone to make sure they are okay.

Sue sits at the bar in full view of all who would want to look, waiting for her friend to arrive. To kill time, she makes a quick call on her phone and talks to her boss for a few minutes. He will pick her up from home tomorrow for work. She then ends the call and runs her hand through her long, blond hair while she looks at the notice board near her and reads the advert about the Guardian Angel group. It gives much detail on why the group has been formed and also mentions some of the members in different towns across the north of England who have joined the group to help the community. Sue then reads a summary of the success that the scheme has had in America, and she is impressed.

The pub is sparsely populated tonight but there are three young lads playing snooker in the middle of the room, close to Sue. Jack, the barman quietly washes some glasses while keeping an eye on everyone in the pub.

In one corner of the pub there is a middle aged, unshaven man in black clothes reading a magazine while keeping out of sight. He has loose black trousers, a black trench coat and a black cap. While keeping his own company he sups a pint of pale ale and notices Sue with her long blond hair. The black capped man then glances at the other youngsters around.

In the opposite corner of the pub is a young, well-built lad wearing an American red and white US jacket, tight blue jeans, trendy trainers and a Chicago cap. The barman shares a joke with him as he brings a drink to his table. The US jacket man then continues to people watch. He sees Sue, notices that she has long blond hair and then takes a look at the other youngsters around.

Sue now hears the bar man talking to him as he has noticed his US Jacket and so mentions the American success of the Guardian Angel project. Sue's mind is soon distracted though, by a fly pestering her juice drink on the bar.

Sue waves the fly away and continues to wait for her friend while she sits at the bar. She doesn't realise that her friend won't make it tonight as she is ill and has forgotten to text Sue to tell her that she won't be able to get to the pub. Sue now sits at the bar on her own, sipping her drink, with her long blond hair glistening from the overhead bar lights. While she sits at the centre of the bar the black capped man and the US jacket man sitting at opposite ends of the pub are both giving her the occasional look.

Then from behind the bar, Jack mentions to one of the snooker lads in a broad Scottish accent that that he is just going outside at the back to change a barrel. He then walks quietly out to the back courtyard.

Eventually, Sue realises that her friend is unlikely to turn up so she decides to go home before one of the three snooker lads tries to chat her up. She gets up and leaves the pub, armed with a raincoat and a small umbrella. It is dark and the rain has stopped now, but it is still damp and the cold winter mist has just started to descend.

As she leaves, she is unaware that the Dark Stalker will be following her tonight.

Once Sue leaves the pub, the black capped man immediately gets up without a sound. He grunts to himself, and follows Sue down the street. As if by reaction, the red and white US jacket man gets up, leaves the pub and follows the black capped man, who is in turn following Sue.

Left in the pub are the three snooker players. They don't know who the other man is who left the pub but they have seen the Guardian Angel get up and leave so they are sure that Sue will be ok. The three of them go to the bar for a drink but Jack has not returned yet, so Molly serves them. Jack eventually returns from the back courtyard a few minutes later and sees that Sue has left her lipstick on the bar. He picks it up, gets his coat and walks outside in an attempt to return it to her. In the misty street he can't see the blond girl, or anyone else for that matter. Then he remembers that he knows where she lives as she had told her boss on the phone earlier. He listens to everything.

Sue has already walked down the misty street and turned left, oblivious to the black capped man who is twenty meters behind her, and the US red and white jacket man who is twenty meters behind him. No one else is anywhere near the three of them on this wintry night and the visibility is now very poor.

Sue walks past the last set of closed shops on the street and makes her way down the dark alley that she knows well. The blacked capped man follows her and the US-jacket man follows him, watching carefully. The black capped man suddenly realises that there is someone behind him, but he keeps his cool.

At the end of the alley Sue reaches a street, turns right and as the black capped man follows her he realises that the US-jacket man behind him has now stopped following and has disappeared. He wonders where he went, but then smiles to himself as it is just him and the blond girl now.

The black capped man starts to slowly close the gap between himself and Sue. He knows her name now because he had earlier heard Sue talking to her boss on her phone in the pub.

Sue now senses that there is someone behind her. She didn't take any notice of the newspaper and radio warnings to avoid dark public parks, thinking that she could look after herself, but she is now petrified.

Sue needs to cross the dark, empty recreation park to get home. The path is narrow and the park is large with no lights, she only has the dim moonlight to see ahead through the mist. She knows that it is a mistake to continue but has no option, as it's the only way home. She feels that there is danger now, and as a number of strange thoughts go through her mind she also remembers that she has left her lipstick on the bar in the pub.

The vulnerable blond girl continues to walk across the dark park, and in front of her at a distance she sees through the mist a faint figure of a man at the park exit gate, under one of the few lights that the park has. She can't tell who it is though.

Sue is really worried as there are men now both in front of her and behind her, and she doesn't know either of them.

As she walks further towards the exit gate she realises that the faint figure of a man in front is in fact the US red and white jacket man standing at the park exit gate. He is about a hundred meters away. She is relieved now and remembers the poster on the noticeboard in the pub about the Guardian Angels and how successful they were in America.

However, she then senses the black capped man behind is getting very near.

Will the killer get her or will the Guardian Angel be in time to save her?

The black capped man behind Sue is very close now as she crosses the dark park. He gets to within two meters of her and feels a throb in his trousers.

Sue panics and walks faster to get to the US red and white jacket man in front of her at the exit gate. He is still a long way off though and the black capped man walks even quicker from behind to catch her up. He whispers her name quietly to her as he puts his hand on her shoulder.

Sue jumps and her heart misses a beat. Then she looks behind at him.

The black capped man tells her not to worry. He pulls out a card and it's a Guardian Angel member card with his photo identity on it. He tells Sue that his name is Fred and offers to escort her home. As he does this he feels another throb in his trousers from a text on his iPhone.

His Guardian Angel leader has sent him the text and he reads it out aloud to Sue in the middle of the dark park.

He reads, "Fred, the police now have an ID for the serial killer. He is wearing a US red and white jacket, tight blue jeans, trendy trainers and a Chicago cap. Beware!!!"

They both look up in front of them through the mist at the park exit gate. The US jacket man has now gone.

That was a close call, thinks Fred and escorts Sue home.

Short Story 3:
The Glass Makers Delight

Victor is a keen gardener. Gardening is his main hobby and, as he has a large garden behind his house, he enjoys making the most of his passion. Victor also works at the glassblowing factory in Pangbury, which helps him to finance his enthusiasm for gardening. He loves spending most of his spare time in the garden and little detracts from his fun. Even his minor ailments don't deter him. He fell off a ladder and twisted an ankle last month which left him hobbling. Then last week, when picking up some broken glass he got a nasty cut deep down the middle finger which needed two hospital cross stiches. Still, as far as Victor is concerned, as long as his back is in good shape then nothing will keep him from his tulips. Even his little forays into playing the odd game of cricket haven't upset his back too much. So, life is reasonably good for Victor, especially as he has won another cricket bet at the town's betting shop. What he hasn't realised yet is that one of his hobbies will soon lead him to being caught out by the police.

Of course, Victor has to spend most of his time earning money to pay for his fun time. This is achieved by working at the glass blowing factory. The company makes premium, expensive glass vases. Some are sold in the UK but many are sent to the USA as they love this kind of ornament and will pay much more than the Europeans. He is one of five expert glass blowers and has been working there for many years. The vases that he makes are the best in the company, and probably the best in the country, which is why he has been there for so long. He also knows the layout of the factory like the back of his hand, which will be useful for the sneaky little scheme he is planning.

The valuable vases produced in the factory are the ones that are later hand painted for the USA market. Only the perfectly crafted vases get to this stage and they are then stored in the locked Red Room. This room is a compact storage area that acts as a show room where each vase has its own pedestal until it is bought by a customer. Before it gets to a pedestal, each vase is alcohol washed so that it gleams clean while perched on the velvet pedestal in the Red Room. Everyone in the factory wears thin disposable gloves so the glassware is kept clean. There are forty expensive finished vases in the Red Room at the moment. They all sit on the main bench, which is dusty but sturdy in contrast to the spotless clean velvet pedestals that sit on it, with their gleaming vases perched on top.

This room contains all the valuable stock and Brian looks after the only key. Brian is the Factory Manager. He will only give the key to someone else if they are asked to do a particular job in the Red Room.

Victor's sneaky idea is that he has found a way of stealing a vase without anyone finding out. He thinks it is fool proof and, as he has been there many years, he knows the company's ways of working and how to use this knowledge to his advantage.

He will quickly make a simple cheap vase, similar to the expensive one that he is targeting which sits in the Red Room. He will then get the key from Brian when he is asked to go in, and replace the valuable vase in the Red room with his simple, cheap one which looks similar. He should then be able to smuggle the desired vase out of the factory when he leaves work. If anyone goes into the room after him they will have to look hard to spot the difference between the one he has stolen and the cheap one he has replaced it with. He will also leave a cigarette stub on the floor to incriminate Bruce, who is one of the other glassblowers, and is the only smoker in the company. As there are forty vases in the Red Room it is unlikely that someone will spot the switch until they are asked to get that particular one from the room. By then he will have sold the vase that he has taken and Bruce will get the rap, for being the only smoker.

The day comes when Victor thinks he can do the steal. He knows Brian wants someone to go into the Red Room today to check the vases are okay and he hopes that will be him. It is perfect timing as Bruce went in the Red Room earlier in the day. Bruce has a criminal record so he will get the blame for today's activities.

Brian does indeed want Victor to do a job in the Red room and has now given him the key to check on the smoke alarm, so he gets the chance to go into the room.

Victor uses the key to get in and closes the door behind him. His thin disposable gloves will ensure there are no fingerprints. He places a used cigarette stub on the floor to incriminate Bruce. Then he quickly checks that the smoke alarm is okay before finding the vase that he wants to steal and do the switch. To do the switch he replaces the vase that he wants, with the cheap look-a-like that he has taken into the room. Everything seems to be going well, but as he reaches to pick up the desired vase he slips slightly on the floor, and knocks the next-door vase with his elbow. Thankfully it doesn't fall but moves out of place slightly on the pedestal, and he recovers his balance by propping himself up on the dusty bench with his hand, and then he repositions the knocked vase. Then he realises that his hand touched the bench and then with dusty fingers he repositioned the adjacent vase. He can now see a dusty finger-mark on it but he is not concerned as he is wearing the universal disposable gloves that they all wear, so no-one will identify the mark as his. Besides, Bruce, who came in earlier in the day, is known to be clumsy so will get the blame.

Victor recovers his poise and listens to hear if anyone has heard him. No-one seems to be aware, thank goodness, and he leaves the room with his desired vase and returns the key to Brian. He takes the vase straight to his car, knowing that the other workers are busy and won't know what he is up to. Job done.

However, Brian has now decided to go into the Red Room himself because an American customer has just phoned with an interest in one of the vases. Brian uses the key to go into the Red Room, only twenty minutes after Victor had done so. Luck is not with Victor as the vase that Brian needs to check on for the American client is in fact the one that Victor knocked with his elbow and then repositioned. Brian is now in front of that vase and can see that next to it is a cheap, fake vase, the one that Victor switched. He can also see that the vase that the American customer is interested in has been repositioned and now has a dusty mark on it. Brian realises that a switch has been made and the valuable vase next door to this one has been stolen. It makes sense to Brian that whoever left that dusty mark on the vase in front of him has stolen the vase next door to it.

Brian knows that all the workers wear thin gloves so there will be no fingerprints anywhere in the room. He steps back and thinks to himself. Only Victor and Bruce have been in here today and he is sure that the cheap fake vase wasn't there yesterday, so it must have been one of them who took it, sometime today. He is not sure who though, but suspects Bruce, as he has a criminal record.

Brian sees a cigarette stub on the floor. He knows that Bruce smokes and that he is also very clumsy, so he thinks that Bruce might have knocked the vase. If he is right he will go to the police.

Then, he notices that there is no ash in the room, either on the floor or on any part of the bench. That is unusual, thinks Brian, you can't smoke a cigarette without losing some ash. So Brian guesses that the cigarette stub has been planted to incriminate the only smoker, which is Bruce. Brian now concludes that if the cigarette was planted in the room then it isn't Bruce who is the burglar, so it must be Victor who has taken the vase. But Brian isn't sure how to prove it.

Brian reckons that as all the glassblowers wear gloves the culprit will have known that there will be no fingerprints left anywhere in the room, so he will think he can get away with it. Then he takes a closer look at the dusty mark on the vase left by the gloved hand of the villain. As expected, the dusty mark has no classic, circular fingerprints which would be left by a naked finger, the glove has prevented that.

However, Brian sees that the dusty finger-mark on the vase is from a finger which has left a slight impression in the dust. The impression shows a single line running down the centre of a finger with two cross marks. These cross marks look like cross stitches to Brian, and he knows that there is only one worker who has stitches on a finger.

Hard luck Victor, you shouldn't have been a gardener.

Short Story 4: Show Me Yours and I'll Show You Mine

Victoria and Wally are not your usual married couple. They have been married for twenty years now and are both in their mid-forties, yet their newfound relaxed attitude to their marriage would probably raise a few eyebrows. They both earn well in their jobs and now own an expensive house in London, so life is comfortable for them.

Wally has just completed his stint on jury service on this wet December day and has been down the pub with his buddy Bill for a quick drink. Bill completed his jury service last year where he and his jury partners found a lad guilty of minor theft. Wally has talked him through his jury session of today, where he and the other jury members convicted a young man on four counts of horrific violent murder, over a three-month period. It even got in the papers. Wally told Bill that he found it incredible that the man's defence team let him go to court sporting a purple Mohican haircut and a scar over his right eye. Bill laughed and thought it was inevitable then that the jury would convict the man looking like that. He then reflected that the lad at his jury service last year looked as bland as you could imagine, with a boring 1980's mullet haircut. They laughed as they shared thoughts over a beer or two and then Wally walked clumsily back home.

Meanwhile, Wally's wife Victoria has had an even more eventful week. She has just returned from a conference in Dubai after speaking on the environmental consequences of cosmetic industry waste products. She is an active environmental campaigner and her presentation made a big impact to her listeners. Victoria got a standing ovation and also an award for her work over the years.

Now that Wally and Victoria are both back from their sessions with jury service and Dubai they are due to have a catch-up, or download as Victoria calls it. This is because they have both played a particular game, a few weeks ago, and now is the time to compare notes.

Prior to this game, they had what most people would call a normal marriage. Over this period of twenty years they had both seemingly been devoted to each other and they at least claimed to be monogamous. However, a few months ago, over a bottle or two of wine, Victoria suggested that to spice things up perhaps they should play a game. Wally was keen to know what type of game she was thinking of. The game Victoria had in mind was inspired from a recent Facebook request she had received a few weeks ago from her first ever boyfriend. Victoria suggested that she and Wally individually and privately look online for a date with someone they have never met before. Rules of the game would be that they can have one evening with whoever they like, no barriers, perhaps with an online profile which would be different to their normal taste in the opposite sex. Victoria clarified that "one evening" meant an evening dinner only and nothing else. Then, when they had both completed their respective dates Victoria and Wally would have an evening meal themselves with of course a bottle of wine, where they would download and share with each other details of their respective evenings.

Wally was surprised initially at Victoria's idea but then thought it would be fun to have dinner with a different charming lady, so a couple of months ago on a warm October night they both spent an evening finding an online dating website to find a partner.

At the time, Wally's attempt to find someone for a dinner date was feeble. He struggled with the online dating agency that he had registered with and couldn't find anyone suitable from the descriptions that he saw on the website. But he had an idea, and went to see his brother Phil who is single and has spent his life having online dates, so Wally thought he would have some tips for him.

Phil is very different to Wally. For a start Phil is exceptionally good looking and has no intention of marrying anyone, but instead wants to have fun with whoever is keen, until he drops dead. Wally once had Phil over to the house for an evening meal to meet Victoria, so they know his attitude. They tried to persuade Phil during the meal to get a soulmate, but Phil just smiled and in his smooth-talking way simply joked saying that Victoria would be the only one he would consider for date!

Phil was indeed a helpful hand for Wally at finding a date online and at last Wally found a someone who was keen to have dinner with him.

Wally noticed that Victoria found no problems finding a date. It seemed to take her only a moment or two to announce that she had had found someone that suited. Wally was impressed, but then again, she was a classy lady.

Of course, neither of them were allowed to know any more details until they had had their download evening, where they would "compare notes" after they had both completed their individual dates.

Then, a few weeks ago, on a November Tuesday evening it was Victoria's turn to meet her date, which was in a posh restaurant that Wally had never heard of, a good twenty-minute drive away. Wally waited up for Victoria to return, which she did just before midnight. He found this evening to be a strange one on his own at home. Having your other half go on a date seemed a bit dangerous. What if Victoria liked him and wanted some more! He had been thinking about this all night and was relieved to see her back when she returned. He asked Victoria what the mystery man was like but she reminded him that the download wasn't until Wally himself had completed his date.

A week later Wally was ready for his date and it was Victoria's turn to have weird feelings in her stomach while her husband was away on a date. Wally went to a local pub to meet his mystery partner. While Wally was in the pub he wandered why Victoria didn't use this pub for her date. It would have been easier for her to come here, he thought, and she would know that Wally wouldn't just wander in to have a peek, as that wasn't part of the "game". He wandered if she was up to something, or perhaps she just wanted a change from the norm.

Wally returned from his date and Victoria noticed he was back earlier than expected, at about eleven o'clock. Perhaps he didn't like his date much she thought, and hoped.

It's now December time and over the last few days, while Victoria was at the conference, Wally and Victoria have kept quiet about their respective dates and have chosen tonight to download what their mystery partners were like when they met them last month.

They have both just prepared a hearty meal and opened a bottle of wine, with some romantic candles. They both sit down to eat and Victoria suggests that Wally starts first.

Wally is indeed happy to go first and says that his date was a completely different type of person to that of Victoria, as Victoria had suggested. He went for a younger girl, ten years younger than Victoria. Her name was Carol and she had short black hair and long slender legs. He shows Victoria a photo. Victoria thinks that Carol looks great and is visually completely the opposite to herself, who has long blond hair and is much shorter than Carol. Victoria is impressed with Wally, having chosen what seems to her to be a very smart girl, and asks him why he came home early after an evening with this stunning girl. Wally replies that the girl had to pick her daughter up from somewhere.

Wally then tells Victoria that it is her turn to spill the beans.

Victoria now gets nervous and starts to describe her evening.

She fidgets.

Victoria says that she went for a twenty-minute drive just in case Wally decided to follow her, as he might not approve of the person she had dinner with.

Victoria looks at Wally.

Wally looks concerned.

Victoria describes the pub décor. Then she talks about the food they had.

But Wally just wants to know about the man.

Victoria slowly starts to describe the man.

Wally's stomach goes cold and his face is sheet white as Victoria describes the man, who had a purple Mohican haircut and a scar over his right eye.

Victoria had not read the papers.

Short Story 5: The Kayak

Phil and Julie Walton are accomplished riders of the kayak. They have now been married for twenty-one years and have kept fit over time, mainly by rowing of some sort. Sometimes they row with their rowing club, but usually they use their two kayaks to take the water. Kayaking is fun, but it can be dangerous, very dangerous.

Phil is a senior insurance broker and is well paid. Being high up in insurance means he can organise the best top class insurance for their cars, home, life and phones. He is short, stocky and keeps fit in the gym, working hard on his shoulders to keep them strong for kayaking. Phil is hardworking and dedicated at work, taking no prisoners, which is why he makes so much money. He has a dark side to his character at work that Julie is unaware of, but he does look after Julie well at home both financially and in their relationship.

Similarly, Julie is no pushover. She is tall, thin and physically fit. She kayaks and also finds time for her other desire, golf. Julie is the manager at the local high street jewellers shop, so has a good head for numbers.

They were married in 1999 and eventually decided not to have children. Their lifestyle means that they are comfortable both financially and with life generally. Riding on the water is a way of life for them and they specialise in kayaking. They practiced hard, were recognised and became the English representatives in the Commonwealth games in the 1990's, so they are experts.

Living in Oxfordshire means they have great access to the river Thames to kayak. This is convenient but hardly a challenge. Even going against the current after heavy rainfall isn't too much for them. The big challenge is the Corryvreckan whirlpool, on the west coast of Scotland. This whirlpool exists between the islands of Jura and Scarba. The roar of the whirlpool is so loud it can be heard ten miles away; it has taken the lives of people in motorboats never mind kayaks. That doesn't bother Phil and Julie. They have been there every year for the last eight years and love the challenge of skirting the whirlpool. They don't actually go through it, but skirt it and flirt with the danger on the perimeter. That's their adrenaline rush.

For the last eight years they have contacted Bruce Burns to arrange their long weekends in Scotland. Bruce, a Corryvreckan local, is employed to keep an eye on the adjacent land to the estuary where the whirlpool is, and also run the boat hiring company on the shore which has the nearest access to the whirlpool. He arranges Phil and Julie's hotel and the hire of kayaks for them, which saves them taking their own (it's hard to carry a kayak on an aircraft). Phil and Julie are wealthy so they pay him well to organise their long weekends, which includes a nice meal for the three of them in the evenings, and of course a wee dram.

Bruce is a classic Scot. He loves his whisky and is a meat eater, as he calls himself. Only the soft English eat vegetables, he thinks. Tall, ageing, with long black hair and a weathered face he is a fisherman by trade and has an old rusty boat to do the local fishing that keeps him financially afloat. He runs the boat hiring company on the shore which allows a maximum of twenty people to canoe or kayak in the bay. His dream is to own his own big fishing trawler, but they cost over ninety thousand pounds and realises this is unlikely, so his realistic dream is to visit Barbados for a few weeks and soak up the sun. He should be able to find the three thousand pounds to fund that at some stage.

On the occasions that Phil has flown to Glasgow for work he has invited Bruce over to enjoy an evening of beers and haggis. A pleasant way to say thanks to an old friend.

Julie also separately visits Edinburgh occasionally, usually with her Oxford lady golfing partner for some 'retail therapy'. The two ladies usually invite Bruce over later in the evening for something to eat as he is a bit of an entertainer with his stories. Bruce isn't well off so appreciates the lavish, all-expenses-paid evening with them.

Bruce does enjoy his separate meetups with Phil and Julie, but only really because they pay for everything, and by everything that means food, booze and the occasional overnight stop in Glasgow with Phil.

Phil and Julie also know that Bruce will organise a good time when they both come up together for their many long weekends kayaking. Eight years of doing that have been great fun. However, things will turn darker for the Waltons soon.

Phil is devious and his ultimate aim is to own a small island off the Scottish coastline and for that he needs serious money, which he has known for some time. Over the years he has devised a plan to get this money. Visiting Corryvreckan started off as a great way to tackle a sporting kayak challenge. Then, after a few years of taking weekends up there in this quiet, relatively uninhabited area, he came up with the plan to generate the money he needed to buy the Scottish island. He was inspired by their life insurance plan annual statement, which came in the post recently and this gave him an idea. Being an insurance expert and having top class life insurance for both of them meant that if an 'accident' was to happen to his wife on Corryvreckan, especially as the risks are understandably high, then the top rate life insurance would pay out well for Phil. He had made sure holidays were included in the insurance. Now that Phil and Julie have been going to Corryvreckan for eight years any 'accident' would not seem suspicious.

So, Phil thinks that the next visit will be the one to create the 'accident' and make him rich. He will talk to Bruce today on the phone to arrange the weekend. Today is a good day to talk to him because Julie is travelling back with her friend from a weekend of shopping in Edinburgh. She is not around so he can talk freely to Bruce.

Phil calls Bruce and offers him £50,000 for his silence and to make sure no one hires any boats on the Saturday that Phil and Julie will go kayaking. That way no one will see Phil do the dirty deed while they are skirting the whirlpool. Bruce jumps at the idea of making so much money. He has no scruples. He might not be able to buy a new trawler but can do a few visits to Barbados with that much money. He even advises Phil on the best way to do the dirty deed. He suggests that a good, precise, horizontal swing with the kayak oar will knock Julie off balance and the turbulent whirlpool will do the rest. Any marks on Julie's head would be thought to be from the whirlpool rocks, when investigated.

Phil has big strong shoulders so could easily deliver such a blow with the oar. All he has to do is practice what Bruce describes as a good precise horizontal swing.

The weekend is set for the middle of June. This means plenty of sunlight for a late-in-the-day accident. When the weekend is nigh, a quick call on the Thursday night to Bruce tells Phil that everything is in place. The car hire is sorted, the hotel is booked for the night before and the bay will be free of people on the Saturday. Phil has transferred the 'accident' money to Bruce. The plan is afoot.

On the Friday afternoon of June 14th Phil and Julie catch a taxi to Heathrow and take their flight to Glasgow, which is on time. They then find the hire car and after and hour of driving they get to the hotel near the bay in good time for something to eat and a beer with Bruce. All is set.

The next day is Saturday which provides a warm clear day. Perfect for kayaking. They can see from the shore of the bay how the water gets choppy, and further in the distance the rapids of the whirlpool developing. Phil and Julie have breakfasted well as Phil has mentioned that lunch won't come for some time when they are on the water (and not at all for Julie today he muses).

They don their life jackets, which to be fair are useful in a river but less use in a whirlpool if you capsize. Bruce stands on the shore pebbles and watches them embarking on their journey out, leaving the shore and moving towards the rapid water. Phil in his kayak looks over his shoulder back to Bruce and smiles. Bruce returns the smile.

Bruce walks back and makes a coffee on his gas stove on the pebbled shore while he watches the two of them row out to the whirlpool in the distance. He loves sweet coffee. Phil previously told him that he won't do the dirty deed for thirty minutes or so, otherwise it might seem suspicious, so Bruce enjoys his sweet coffee and garibaldi biscuit. Forty minutes later Bruce gets his binoculars out and peers through them. He watches Phil and Julie near the rapids. Sure enough, there goes the precise horizontal swing of the oar and the subsequent capsize of the kayak. Job done. The lone kayaker returns towards Bruce. Bruce smiles as the pound signs go through his mind. How can making so much money be so easy he thinks?

As the lonely kayaker approaches the shallows Bruce calls out. "That went to plan then."

"Yes, perfect" replies Julie. "We make a great team Bruce".

It wasn't just Phil who was inspired months ago by the annual statement of their joint insurance plans, which came in the post. Julie got a similar idea. Two minds think alike.

Bruce thinks back to the visits that Julie made to Edinburgh to see him, with her golfing friend. Bruce regularly met with them and on the last occasion Julie suggested the plan for Phil to have an 'accident'. It was no coincidence that she made him an offer a few days after Phil's offer. They had both seen the insurance statements in the post on the same day and Julie, being a golfer, has great timing so can deliver a good horizontal blow without trying too hard.

Julie is almost back at the shore now.

Bruce looks up to Julie as she enters the shallows.

"Wait" he says. "Look back there. Phil's lone boat has returned to its upright state and is caught in some seaweed. Your swing was so strong that the kayak capsized and now has swivelled back upright again. Before we call the authorities to tell them of the accident you need to make sure it's inverted, which it would be if he had accidentally capsized."

Julie looks back. "Dam, you are right Bruce, well spotted. I will go and turn it over".

Bruce responds. "You'll need help, the current is picking up and the seaweed is tangling the boat up." He quickly gets his lifejacket on and drags his own kayak to the shore.

Together they both go out to fix the problem. As they go back out Julie smiles to herself and thinks of the money she will get from Phil's demise.

The next day is a bright, fine, blue-sky day, similar to the previous one.

Bruce is sitting on the shore reading the local papers while having a coffee. The news is front page.

On Saturday at about midday Philip Walton, an experienced Oxford kayaker lost his life when the whirlpool at Corryvreckan consumed his boat and took his life. His wife Julie and their event organiser Bruce Burns went to assist, but in the attempt to rescue Phil Julie also lost her life. An investigation is in place with the authorities.

Bruce leans back in his chair. He also plays golf and can deliver a precise horizontal swing with his oar, this time for Julie.

He muses to himself. £50,000 from Phil and £60,000 from Julie means that he can now buy his trawler and also go to Barbados. With Julie out of the picture as well, then there's no one to grass him up to the police.

His coffee tasted sweet.

Short Story 6: The Scam

Scammers are horrible people. The worst kind are those who ring elderly people up and pretend to be from their bank, encouraging them to hand over their personal data and then getting access to their savings. They are then robbed of their money. In addition, these scammers often live relatively near their victims. That's not what neighbourhood watch should be about.

There are of course many other ways to scam people. The three Hunter brothers are rogue builders in their early thirties who travel around southeast England housing estates. They knock on people's doors hoping to find an elderly vulnerable person and then tell them that a roof tile is loose and they can fix it for them. They estimate the cost to be £80 and then ultimately charge £300 for the work, which only takes five minutes. It sounds a mild, harmless scam, or fraud, but if they get challenged then the Hunters become angry and intimidating, until payment is made. Also, while one of them is on the roof the other two are inside the house taking advantage of the elderly persons generosity for a cup of tea. They then look around the house and secretly steal small, valuable items from the house. They are vile people, as are all scammers and fraudsters.

This scenario is exactly what happened in Surbiton's Rose Avenue, a quiet neighbourhood where Fred lives at number eighty-two, at the corner of the street.

Fred has just retired from work for health reasons at the age of sixty-six. He hobbles around his house with his dodgy hip, while a mild stroke last year makes his cognitive skills slightly below par. His hobby in retirement is to make ornaments from soft cork wood. He has a cutting machine in his shed and takes hunks of cork and makes various ornaments such as kitchen coasters, mats, plugs, and bottle stoppers etc. It helps to pass the time of day for him.

As he is retired Fred can now look after a dog and has recently been given Patch. Patch is a Springer Spaniel bitch and came from his next-door neighbour recently who was getting another younger dog. That suited Fred well as he needs company now that he doesn't have to go to work and he lives alone.

Fred is aware that the Hunter brothers have just visited his old friend Jack further up the street at number forty, but he doesn't know that they are bad people and they will eventually fleece him for £300.

Fred had earlier walked Patch and as they walked past Jacks house Fred stopped by the Hunters VW transit van and chatted to one of the brothers to make polite conversation, while Patch sat and simply stared at his new owner. The Hunters took note of Jack for future reference. He would be an easy victim. Jack was intrigued by their VW van as he had also recently bought a similar van for his cork ornament work, and the Hunters van seems well set up inside to cater for their tools. This has given him some ideas on how to set up his own van. He might go to B&Q during this week he thinks. Fred finishes his pleasant conversation with one of the Hunters, says a polite goodbye, then continues the walk with Patch. This is how scammers work. They are pleasant and engaging, to lure you in initially, and then they strike.

Later in the day the three brothers look for another victim in the street, and they are looking at Fred's house now that he is back home, and think this is an easy job. One of them drives the van over to Fred's house and the other two walk over and knock at Fred's door.

Fred is hard of hearing but just about hears the doorbell while in the kitchen making coffee. His hip aches badly now but he hobbles to the door and sees the three Hunter brothers standing together, all smiling. One of them is charming and explains that one of Fred's roof tiles is loose and they can fix it for £80.

It sounds a good deal and Fred agrees. One of the Hunter brothers pleasantly offers to help Fred hobble back to his kitchen. Fred gives thanks for the help and two brothers are invited in for a cuppa while the other one gets the big ladder from their VW Transit Van and gets on the roof.

The two brothers look around Fred's house while escorting to him to the kitchen. They can see radios, an iPad, a crystal vase, an iPhone, a wallet and a Rolex watch. All will be easy to steal. They can tell from Fred's doddery manner that he won't notice the disappearance of these items for a while. They can also see from the notes peeking out from Fred's wallet that he has enough cash to pay the £300 that they will soon demand. Their typical plan is being executed well.

The other brother has been on the roof doing nothing for ten minutes and then comes down and claims that the tile is fixed. He then, instead of the agreed £80, charges Fred £300 while his brothers are standing alongside him, a trio of nastiness, as if daring Fred to refuse.

Fred meekly challenges them as they have charged more than they originally quoted. They get angry and let Fred know what will happen if they don't get their £300. That's not what neighbourhood watch should be about, Fred thinks.

Fred looks over at his wallet and tells them that he will pay but will need to send a text to his sister to ask her to transfer twenty pounds to him or he won't have food for the week. He goes over to pick up his wallet and the iPhone, then sends a text. One of the brothers goes outside to put the ladder back in the van, now that they know they will be paid.

The other two brothers go to the van for a cigarette and Fred joins them by the van with his wallet. Patch wanders out with him and as he gets to the van to talk to the two smoking brothers Patch sits down and looks at Fred. Fred smiles at patch and then gets his wallet out from his pocket.

As he does this the three brothers are now all at the van with Fred, waiting for him to get the cash out from his wallet.

Fred looks up at them and stalls for time. The three men look very intimidating.

They return his look with three gruesome stares in impatience as they know Fred is now wasting their time. One of the brothers gets his iPhone out and types something, which worries Fred.

The elder brother demands the money again. Fred looks at his wallet and then looks at the elder brother again. One of the other brothers repeats the demand.

Fred looks at his wallet yet again, while Patch sits there looking at Fred with a sorry look on his face.

The third brother tells Fred what will happen if he doesn't get a move on, but Fred keeps stalling.

Then it all happens. A screech of tyres is heard by all of them as an old black Mercedes car comes around the corner of the street and slams its brakes on within a metre of them all. Fred's heart misses a beat.

Mrs. Smart at number seventy, lives opposite Fred and looks through her window at the scene and fears for Fred. She has been watching for the last five minutes and is worried for Fred's safety but can do nothing about it. She wandered who one of the brothers was texting and now it appears to her to be some sort of back up. She now looks at the car which has just screeched its tyres in stopping, and the two men inside the car waering black leather jackets do not look pleased. She hopes the thugs haven't come to beat Fred up. Fred's dog Patch is only a spaniel and is too small to protect him. This isn't what neighbourhood watch is about, she thinks.

The two men get out of the car and come over to the Hunters and Fred, who are standing by the VW van. One of them is wearing a red cap. He has a massive scar over his left eye and stares at Patch, who was originally looking at Fred and now looks at the angry man with the red cap. He is called Kurt.

Kurt is Fred's next-door neighbour, the man who gave Patch to Fred for his retirement as Kurt was getting another younger drug sniffer dog in his work as a Police drug enforcement officer. Patch, a now retired drug sniffer dog, is glad to see him again but doesn't greet Kurt in the way that a dog usually does. He just simply stares at him. When he does this Kurt knows it means that Patch has found Class A narcotic drugs. Fred had already sensed this from Patch earlier in the day when Patch had sat down and stared at him while Fred was talking to the Hunters, as they walked by their van earlier in the day. So, Fred had already worked out that the Hunter brothers were carrying drugs.

When they came to his door to offer to fix the tile, Fred guessed they would get difficult. So, when Fred got challenged by the Hunters in his kitchen to pay £300 he didn't text his sister for money but texted Kurt instead about the presence of the Hunters and the drugs.

Kurt and his police partner now look in the van and body-search all three brothers. One of them has drugs on him so he is arrested.

Fred has a buzzing in his trousers and looks at his iPhone. His Find-My-Phone app is telling him where his stolen iPad is and it is now in the van. Fred tells Kurt, who looks in the van, retrieves it and arrests one of the other brothers for theft.

These two brothers are handcuffed and bundled in the unmarked Mercedes police car. Kurt drives them away to the station.

The third brother is told by Kurt's police partner to sit in the passenger seat of his VW van while the policeman drives him and the van away to be examined by the police.

However, as soon as the policeman starts the engine they go no more than half a meter when the engine goes bang and the end-pipe of the exhaust falls off.

Fred walks to the back of the van and picks something up off the road. The policeman gets out and also takes a look at the rear. He shakes his head and tells Fred that criminals never look after their sorry old banger cars and asks Fred if the VW van can be left there until the police can come over with a pickup truck and take it away later today. Fred agrees and the policeman rings Kurt to come back so that they can drive all three Hunter brothers in the Mercedes, and take them to the station.

Back comes the car, they pick up Kurt's partner and the Hunter brother, and then off they all go again to the station. The three criminals will soon be locked up.

Fred stands there on the pavement, now on his own. He gets the object out from his pocket that he found on the road. It's one of his cork plugs, which he stuffed up the exhaust pipe while the brothers were not looking. Fred smiles to himself.

Next to him is their VW transit van. It's similar to his own which is sitting over there on his drive. But the Hunters VW van is full of ladders, tools and other equipment.

Fred takes the tools and ladders out and puts them in his own van.

No need to go to B&Q now.

He also notices in the van the Rolex and crystal vase that they stole from his house, so he retrieves them. He also takes a television, PlayStation, soundbars, three iMacs and four expensive cameras that the hunters stole from various people in his street over the last week. Fred will go on Facebook and tell everyone in the street that he has retrieved these stolen items, for whoever had them stolen by the Hunters.

That's what neighbourhood watch should be about.

Short Story 7: The Savvy Barmaid

She doesn't know it yet, but tonight there will be some excitement for Zoe in the Bonne hotel in Paris. Zoe is the barmaid at the cosy hotel, where guests tend to have a drink in the hotel bar before they move on to find a restaurant in Paris. She is an experienced hotel employee and she is a barmaid with a difference.

Coming from a poor Spanish family in Sunningrad in southern Spain, Zoe is a smart looking, tall, thin, twenty three year old with short black hair. Observant and paying attention to detail, Zoe loves analysing people, which helps if you work in a bar. She knows that guests would complain at the slightest problem, so she prides herself on getting everything right. No-one is going to catch her out, even the hotel manager was impressed. After her first few weeks there were no complaints. Instead there were many compliments, so he nicknamed Zoe "The Boss". It always helps when a barmaid is smart and switched on, and she will need to be both of those tonight.

Another facet to Zoe's armoury is that she reads body language well. She knows when a guest needs a refill and gets to them before they have a chance to ask. She can sense a problem before it happens and always sorts it out with her customary warm smile. But what makes her slick is that a few years ago she learned a few conjuring tricks, which involves sleight of hand. She found this useful occasionally, and would find it particularly useful tonight. After all, she needs to live up to her tag The Boss.

There are some antics that go on in this hotel. This week there have been some minor thefts from rooms and one or two guests have had to have their bags searched by Zoe.

Frequently, in the bar, she sees groups of business lads drinking on expenses and goading each other on to do something ridiculous. There's the occasional business lady who obviously owns her company and wants to be left alone while enjoying a glass of wine and interrogating her mobile phone. Usually though, she sees groups of two or three business people harmlessly wiling away the time in the bar before tomorrow's work day arrives. Typically, the hotel is quiet. Tonight is different though and Zoe will have to be savvy as table six is looking interesting.

At table six an attractive, blond young lady had sat down alone at the table some time ago and Zoe delivered her order with her customary warm smile. A young man joins the lady now. He appears very confident, speaks to the young lady, but does not stay for long. Zoe served this young man last night. He was pig headed and had bragged to Zoe how he could charm the ladies with ease. He said he could get his sister to do what he asked. He even gets his wife to pack and unpack his business suitcase for him. Last night the young man bought drinks for another young lady, until he saw Zoe watching him, so he decided to move on. He then paid Zoe for his drink by cash, which is strange as cash is suspiciously unusual payment nowadays. He is back again tonight.

Zoe looks up and the lady at table six seems concerned now. Has Zoe missed something? She goes over to the lady and senses that she is wearing Chanel no.5 perfume. Zoe asks her if she is okay. The lady replies that she has mislaid a fifty Euro note. Zoe advises that she can pay for her drinks the next morning when she checks out, but now she suspects that the young man has taken money from the lady without her knowing.

Zoe remembers a young lady last night had a similar concerned look on her face when the same young man left her. Perhaps she had also "lost" some money.

Later in the evening the young man returns for his nightcap, having had a night out in Paris. He orders a brandy from Zoe at the bar and pays for it with a fifty Euro note.

Zoe doesn't believe in coincidences so, as she puts it in the till, she sneakily gives it a sniff, and smiles as she senses the hint of Chanel no. 5 perfume. It looks like he took it from the lady so The Boss will sort this out tomorrow morning.

In the morning Zoe is serving coffee in the open plan foyer, adjacent to the bar. She keeps an observant watch. The young man who stole the money last night comes down the stairs, checks out at reception then asks for a coffee. Zoe serves him coffee with her customary warm smile.

"Some nice ladies in last night" offers Zoe.

"Yes, they can't get enough of me" replies the cocky young man laughing.

"I bet you that I can take something from that lady without her seeing." says Zoe glancing over at the lady from last night who 'lost' the money.

The young man laughs, doesn't believe Zoe can do it, but likes a challenge so agrees the wager.

Zoe is now on a bet and walks over to the young lady who has just arrived with her suitcase to check out. They are now at the other end of the coffee bar, out of earshot of the young man, who watches from a distance to see how slick Zoe is. He senses that whatever she is saying to the young lady isn't working as the lady appears upset with her. Zoe has asked to search her suitcase, which she then does and hands it back, apologises for the inconvenience, and leaves the lady, who gives her a very angry, cold look.

Zoe walks back over to the young man and smiles at him, while moving his bag out of the way so she can pass.

"What did you do" asked the young man.

Zoe, still smiling, replies "I told her I needed to search her luggage, and without her seeing, I got this." Zoe carefully reveals the lady's personal diary from her sleight of hand work.

The young man laughs and says "okay you win." He hands over the wager and says "good luck getting the diary back to her without her seeing".

Zoe replies "Don't worry, I am good at sleight of hand. I will easily get it back in her suitcase unseen".

The young man then leaves the hotel.

Zoe wanders back over to the lady.

"Why did you search my case earlier?" the lady asks, still angry.

"Sorry, I'll explain in a minute, but I thought you might like this." Zoe hands her a fifty Euro note, which had been the wager with the young man. The young lady now smiles and says

"You found it then?"

"I got it back it from the young man who stole it from you last night. It had a scent of Chanel no.5 so I knew it was he who stole it from you. Also, I hope you don't mind, but I removed your personal diary from your suitcase to get your money back." Zoe returns her diary to the lady.

The lady smiles. "So it was he who took my money. Should we take him to the police?"

"No need" replies Zoe. "I also took a pair of your black lace knickers from your suitcase. He doesn't know it but they are now hidden in his suitcase. I put them in there when I moved his bag out of the way just now. He told me yesterday that his wife packs and unpacks for him, so he will have more trouble at home with his wife than he would with the police."

The lady is rather taken aback, but then throws back her head and laughs, says thank you, then turns to leave the hotel.

Zoe, with her customary warm smile, watches the lady as she exits the door.

She is The Boss.

Short Story 8: The Coach Ride

Steve is a lucky guy. He has committed a crime, stealing twenty thousand pounds from a post office, but no one can prove it. He even went to court, but the prosecution couldn't prove he committed the crime so he avoided going to jail.

So, life seems good now for Steve. All he has to do is wait and when things have died down he can retrieve the money that he has hidden, which is in a cemetery. However, Steve does silly things and makes mistakes in life occasionally, and he must be careful over the next few days.

A month after being released from court Steve arranges to visit his brother in Cardiff as he hasn't seen him for a while. On the day of the visit Steve gets to Victoria Station and finds the coach which will take him from London to Cardiff. He is happy but starts drinking. It's his only vice nowadays, and it is alcohol which will soon catch him out.

As he boards the coach he greets the driver and as he passes him he notices the driver is wearing a royal blue Wimbledon tennis scarf. Steve loves sport so asks him what the scarf represents. The driver tells him that he is a tennis fan and he is wearing his Wimbledon tennis club scarf, and by the way that is fifteen-love. Steve thinks he is a bit weird, then asks him if he plays tennis nowadays. The driver replies that he plays club tennis occasionally with his mates, and it is now thirty-love, to him. Steve thinks the driver is seriously bonkers and ends the conversation by asking him if he has met anyone famous at Wimbledon. The driver replies by saying that he has met Tim Henman and he also has his autograph, and by the way that is now forty-love. Steve sighs, then walks towards his seat to get away from this mad driver. His seat is just behind the driver and Steve wonders if he really wants to be driven my such a madman.

Steve sits behind the driver in the first set of two seats. The seat next to him is vacant but soon a man called Tom boards the coach and sits next to him. They start chatting and exchange pleasantries. Tom appears normal so Steve is thankful for that. He is the local undertaker and has been busy as Covid has struck recently. Tom is taking a weekend break and visiting his old university friends in Penarth, near Cardiff.

In the seat behind Steve and Tom is a lady in her eighties. She has blue-rinse hair and is wearing very old-fashioned octogenarian clothes, bless her. She is also wearing that ancient rose perfume that old ladies usually wear, the intensity of which annoys Steve as he munches some crisps. In the seat next to the octogenarian lady is a young spotty teenager, but he has quietly nodded off.

A group of ten football fans are at the back of the coach and taunt the driver as he likes tennis and not football. All the football fans support Arsenal and are going to Cardiff for the FA Cup game. Steve loves a taunt so joins the football fans in teasing the bus driver, singing derogatory songs about tennis and Wimbledon and then rude songs about the driver. After all, it's what you do on a coach, he thinks.

During the journey Steve drinks his bottle of scotch. He drinks a little too much for his own good. He gets even more annoyed as he can still smell that rose scented perfume behind him, and now the old lady has started chatting to the young lad which annoys him even more as he slowly gets drunk.

Meanwhile, next to him is Tom who tells Steve that he is looking forward to emigrating to Australia next week. A big move for him. Steve enjoys hearing Tom's plans for moving to Australia. He feels he can now talk to Tom openly as he won't be in the country after next week. He is dying to talk to someone about his stash of money which he stole from the post office, as he hasn't been able to tell anyone yet. In a drunken moment he tells Tom that he has stolen money from the post office and has hidden the twenty thousand pounds. Tom asks him where he has hidden it and now Steve is cocky as well as drunk, so he speaks before he thinks and it slips out of his mouth that he has buried it in the corner of the local cemetery beneath the big oak tree.

As soon as he says it Steve regrets the brag. However, Tom will no longer be in UK after next week so Steve feels that he will get away with his slip up. He glances behind and sees the lady staring out of the window and the young lad appears to be napping again. Steve is not sure if they heard his brag.

The coach gets to Cardiff and they all go their separate ways. Steve visits his brother and has a great day catching up on all that they have missed over the last few months.

He then returns home the next day on the return coach. On the coach back to London he sits on his own as not many people are on the trip to London. He has time to reflect on yesterday and realises he has made a big alcoholic mistake in telling Tom about the hidden money. Tom might want to get hold of it before he goes to Australia. However, Steve still has time to get back to London and dig up the cash before Tom looks for it. Then he thinks more about that coach ride yesterday. There was the lady behind him who may have heard. She might be eighty but her hearing could well be fine. The young lad next to her also might have heard, even though he was engaged in talking to the old lady for much of the time. Steve thinks urgency is now required to move the money from beneath the big oak tree in the cemetery. He rues his alcoholic behaviour.

The following day Steve is having coffee in his kitchen and hears on the radio that Covid lockdown is to be enforced which means all aircraft are to be grounded. He is again angry with himself that he spilled the beans to Tom on the coach. Tom now will not get to Australia so has more time to find Steve's money. Steve has just realised that Tom had mentioned that he was an undertaker, which means he regularly visits the cemetery in his work, so he can be there regularly without suspicion. This is the same cemetery that he hid the money in. Steve decides he must get his money urgently, before Tom gets there. He originally didn't want to dig up the money until much time had passed, but now he must do so quickly before Tom gets to it.

The following evening, under the cover of darkness, Steve makes his way to the cemetery. All is quiet and he is sure no one has followed him, after all who wants to be in a cemetery after dark?

He gets to the oak tree in the corner of the cemetery where the money is buried and sees that there is now a new grave right next to the oak tree. It has fresh soil on top of it. There is also fresh soil in the area by the oak tree where he had hidden his stash of money. Steve's stomach goes cold. He is sure someone has been here and dug up his money. Tom must have been here he thinks. Tom has certainly been at the nearby grave, in a working capacity as an undertaker, so he had the opportunity to get the cash.

Now he is at the oak tree and he gets on his hands and knees to remove the soil and see if his money is still buried there. Steve can smell something in the air. It's the scent of roses. The same smell that annoyed him on the coach. Surely the old lady on the coach hasn't had the energy to come here and go digging. Then Steve looks up and realises that the scent is from a rose bush near the oak tree.

Steve, now relieved that the old lady didn't get the cash, uses his hands to brush the soil away to check if the bag of money is still there.

It has gone, but there is something else there that has replaced the money.

It is a cloth. A royal blue cloth in the shape of a long rectangle. Steve realises it is a scarf and has the words 'Wimbledon Tennis' embroidered on it. There is also a handwritten message that says "Game, set and match".

That pesky driver coach driver took Steve's money.

Short Story 9: Keep it Close to You

Chad calls himself a loser. He had a poor upbringing so he was never going to have a good start to life. He then left home at sixteen and didn't see his parents again. Chad's life revolves around claiming benefits, eating unhealthily, smoking and buying a scratch card every Saturday. A monotonous routine. He has a few friends but none have a good moral standing and, given the choice, you would rather keep a distance from them.

Chad doesn't realise it at the moment but today will have a dramatic ending for him.

Life has never given Chad a break in the past, but today it does. It is a Saturday and at the local newsagent he wins on a scratch card that he has bought, and it is a significant win of five thousand pounds. The newsagent doesn't have the cash to give to him now but, instead, he gives Chad a receipt so he can claim it from the Post Office next door.

Chad goes straight to the Post Office to claim the money. He joins the long queue and while he is waiting he takes a look around him - after all, he will soon have a lot of money and this is the kind of area where you are likely to be mugged. There are two girls walking around the shop whom Chad knows. One, the fiery redhead, is an undesirable, whereas the other seems a pleasant girl. How they enjoy each other's company is a mystery to Chad. He knows the fiery redhead carries a knife occasionally. It is also getting dark outside, so Chad needs to be careful when he leaves.

He is third in the Post Office queue and looking behind him he sees two people. One is a tired looking unsteady old man with a walking stick who has a cute Jack Russell dog. Chad smiles at the dog. Behind the old man is a younger man who lives up the road from Chad. He has a scar across his eye from an incident that saw him go to jail a few years ago. Chad and his friends nicknamed him 'Slasher' because of his scar. Chad only knows of Slasher because they both share the same heart condition, which isn't helped by both of their unhealthy lifestyles. While Chad has a careful diet, this man does not and he knows he will come to regret this in the future.

While Chad stands in the queue he feels that for his safety he needs to avoid both Slasher and the two girls in the post office. However, Slasher shouts to Chad.

"What are you queuing up for?" he asks.

"Err, nothing much" replies Chad, nervous now as Slasher is watching from behind.

Chad gets to the front of the queue. The two girls pay for their items at the other cashier alongside him.

"How can I help you?" the cashier says.

"Err, I would like to claim this please?" Chad says self-consciously handing in the receipt.

The cashier carefully counts out five thousand pounds and hands it over to Chad, in full view of all the other customers. Chad is now worried. It is dark outside and he is concerned that the fiery redheaded girl and Slasher are around to cause trouble. He takes the money, stuffs it in his back pocket, which now bulges, and walks out quickly.

Outside, he starts his walk towards home. He pauses to tie his shoelace, but now the two girls have finished in the shop and are leaving at the same time as he is. Chad fears the worst so needs a potential witness in case of problems. He doesn't know the nice girl, so can't be sure she will help him, if he needs it. Fortunately, the old man and his dog are leaving as well so Chad walks slowly behind both the dog and the man. No-one is going to mug him with an old man and a yapping dog around.

The man and his dog walk slowly in front of Chad while the two girls walk even slower behind him. Too slow for it to be natural, Chad thinks. They can probably see the wedge of money is his back pocket. That was a mistake thinks

Chad, he should have put it in his inside pocket. However, he can't touch it now because if they haven't already seen the bulge, then they will see it if he touches his back pocket. Chad continues to walk behind the old man and his dog, with the girls following close behind him.

Then, Chad hears a male voice further behind him. It is Slasher talking to the redhead. Slasher has finished in the shop and has caught the girls up. Chad hears the redhead tell Slasher that she is watching Chad because he has some money. Chad starts to sweat.

Suddenly the old man turns around and apologises to Chad for being a slow walker. Chad sees an opportunity to stop and talk to the man which will encourage the girls and Slasher to overtake him, walk on and get out of the way. That way he can see them while they are in front, and he will then be aware of what's going on. Chad stops and talks to the old man, taking his time, and sure enough the girls and Slasher walk past him, but not before eyeballing him.

Chad faces the old man and chats to him to waste more time and avoid looking at Slasher.

"You have a nice dog, what's his name?" Chad asks as he turns around and bends down to pat the dog on his head.

"His name is Bonzo" replies the old man who watches Chad take his time patting the dog, while Slasher and the two girls walk further on from them.

"I am new to the area. They look like nasty people" says the old man quietly.

"Yes, thanks for helping me. I suggest that you keep clear of them and make sure you keep your valuables close to you" advises Chad.

The old man thanks Chad for his advice and hobbles off with his dog.

Chad carries on walking. He gets to a dark alley which is the short cut to the road where he lives. The girls are waiting for him in the alley. The nice girl is trying to persuade the redhead to go home but she won't have it. Chad cannot turn around and go back now as that would acknowledge that he has something to hide, so Chad carries on and hopes that the girls will leave him, but he is wrong.

"So, you got some decent money today then?" says the redhead as Chad walks past.

"Never you mind" he says.

Then she shoulder-barges him, and he falters to keep his balance.

"Come on share it around then" she says as she pushes him into the wall and then bear hugs him hoping to find the bulge of his back trouser pocket where she earlier saw the money. Chad muscles his way out of it and runs off instinctively, while she laughs.

The nice girl walks off to go home.

As Chad runs off through to the other end of the alley he sees that Slasher is waiting for him at the far end.

"Come on then. I heard you had money. Hand it over" says Slasher.

"Leave it out buddy, I only have a bit of cash, nothing much"

"Well, that will do, give it to me" and with that they have a tussle. Chad feels Slashers hand grapple around his upper back and then his back trouser pocket, but that's all Chad feels as he loses his senses; he is knocked to the ground and becomes unconscious as his head hits the floor.

Chad wakes up a few hours later in hospital with nasty injuries to his head and with no money. Next to him in a chair is a policeman. He tells Chad that a witness called the police and told them that Chad had been assaulted and the police are now searching for the assailants. However, Chad knows that by the time the police find Slasher and the girls his money will have gone.

The policeman smiles and tells Chad that the police already know of Slasher and the redhead, as they both have a criminal record. They don't know the other girl though. The police are now at their homes searching for all three of them and for anything they might have potentially taken from him. He tells Chad that if they find anything on Slasher then the scar faced man will go to jail for a long time. Chad hopes this is the case.

Chad lies there in the hospital bed with the policeman next to him waiting for him to be fit enough to give a statement. Chad thinks through what happened. He has to work out if it was the redhead or Slasher who took his money. The police will never work it out so he needs to figure out what actually happened in that alley. Did the redhead get the money off him in the tussle or did Slasher? Either way the money will be hidden by now. He thinks to himself that the police would have been too late to find the money at their flats. If it was the redhead who took it in the tussle with him, then she would have hidden it somewhere on her way home. If it was Slasher who took it after he bundled Chad then Slasher would have had time to put it somewhere by now. Mind you, if the police found the money at Slashers house that would be perfect, as Chad would get his money back and Slasher would be jailed for a long time.

The policeman gets a call on his mobile phone. He ends the call and tells Chad that the police didn't find the money at Slasher's flat or the redhead's flat. Chad suspected one of them had hidden the money somewhere on the way home.

The policeman also said that his colleagues interrogated the redhead girl with no success. They couldn't find any trace of the nice girl or of Slasher, who had fled from his house and he hasn't been found yet. The policeman said that for Slasher, only the local park and forest were near enough for him to flee from the police, and they are currently looking for him there, so that hopefully they can arrest him for grievous bodily harm and potential theft. However, Chad is aware that Slasher knows the local park well, so can hide easily.

Chad is angry now while lying in bed with a sore head, and suspects that the redhead might have clobbered Slasher in a scrap for Chads money; or perhaps Slasher's weak heart has failed him and he has had a heart attack. He smiles in hope, and falls asleep as the hospital drugs take effect.

The next morning the policeman has gone.

Chad gets coffee from the nurse and reads the local paper.

In it he reads about an incident in the local park.

A man has died of a heart attack while sitting on a bench in the local children's play park. He was taking a rest when his heart failed and he was found by the community police. On the man was a wad of notes to the tune of five thousand pounds. Near the old man who died was his beloved Jack Russell dog.

Chad's face turned white.

It wasn't Slasher or the girls who mugged him. It was the old man who had taken his money when Chad bent over to pat the dog.

Short Story 10: A Dodgy Day in London

Tom is sitting on the train from Newcastle to London and is thinking of the day out he will have today. He is to meet Jane, his sister, in the big city and he hasn't seen her for three years, so he is excited to see how his little sister is doing.

Tom and Jane were brought up in Newcastle and got on very well together at home while growing up, unusually well for brother and sisters. When they both went to university in different parts of England they missed each other but made friends at their respective universities so that covered for the loss. Tom went to Newcastle University, graduated and has now been working for six months in a law firm. He earns well so is looking forward to treating his little sister to a day out.

Jane, has also just finished university, but in London where she lives now. The move from home was a big culture shock for her. She hasn't managed to get a job yet so is trying to make ends meet while living in London. She has an interview next week though which is encouraging.

Toms train arrives in London and they meet on the platform in a big embrace. They don't waste time and go straight into a coffee shop for a snack and catch up.

Over coffee, Tom looks at Jane and is a little surprised. By the look of her clothes she is clearly struggling for cash, which is to be expected in London if you have no job. Jane tells him that she lives with a friend, Sue, in a flat in what Tom thinks is a run-down part of London. Hopefully Janes interview will be successful for her. Jane shows Tom a photo of her with her flat mate. Tom thinks that they seem like good pals and he hopes Jane is happy. At least she is here now for a great day out with him and her manner suggests that she is clearly happy to see him and looking forward to the day.

Jane is impressed with Toms story. His progression from college to having a job sounds encouraging. He has clearly earned well and likes the idea of being a "big bruv" doting on his little sister. They chat away over their snack and are both sure today will be entertaining.

They catch the tube to Oxford Street and do the tourist walk along the shops, looking at what's on offer and talking at the same time.

At lunch time they take a pizza and rest their legs for a while.

In the afternoon they continue the walk down Oxford Street. They walk past a policeman who advises Tom to put his wallet in an inner jacket pocket and not in his back trouser pocket for all to see. Tom ignores the policeman as he has never had a problem before in Newcastle so why worry today?

Tom and Jane are now on Regent Street and walk past Hamleys toy shop where there are many people in costumes enticing children into the store. Tom gets a hug from a huge seven-foot-tall Mickey Mouse, a man inside a costume of course. He laughs at Mickey as he and Jane walk past, then they watch the excitable kids drag their mums into the store.

Right next to Hamleys is a man selling roasted chestnuts. Jane and Tom love chestnuts so they ask for a bag and wait for a few minutes for the chestnuts to be ready and bagged up. The man is very chatty and soon they have their purchase. Toms takes some loose change out for the man and then they continue the walk.

They walk past a florist and then see another costumed animal, this time Donald Duck on his own, walking back, towards Hamleys. He too gives Tom a long bear hug and walks off in the direction of the Toy shop.

It is then that Tom starts to get uncomfortable as there are now even more people on the streets of London. A pretty girl suddenly walks up to them both and asks Tom if he has the time. Tom looks at his watch and tells her the time, at which point a scruffy man bumps into him from behind. In stumbling, Toms turns around and bumps into the pretty girl. The scruffy man apologises, Tom accepts the apology and suddenly both the man and pretty girl are gone. All part of busy London, Tom thinks.

Jane then suggests a coffee stop as she is tired and needs a caffeine boost. In Costa coffee shop Tom orders the drinks and then realises that his wallet is gone from his back pocket. He tells Jane, who replies that her rail ticket is now missing from her back pocket. He looks at Jane and then he realises that the policeman was right, he should have kept his wallet more secure. Jane pays with the few coins that she has and they sit down to have coffee while Tom rings the bank on his mobile phone to cancel the card from his wallet. The bank tells him that someone has used it already and taken £300.

Tom is furious. He can cope with the money loss as he is well paid but he hates criminals for what they do. He tells Jane he can cover her rail ticket with some cash he has in his inside pocket, as he knows she is generally skint.

Tom glances at the free newspaper on the table that the previous occupant has left and sees the word "stolen" which catches his eye. The article talks about the increase in pickpocketing in the centre of London and that the latest tactic is to work in three's. Here, the first person talks to you, then the second person bumps into you from behind and while you stumble the third person pick-pockets you. Tom realises that that is what happened just now with the pretty girl. He was amazed that the pretty girl and her scruffy accomplice were so slick that Tom didn't realise there was a third person taking his wallet.

While sitting in the coffee shop Tom wonders if there was another way he lost his wallet. He thinks back to what happened earlier in the day to try and work out how his wallet was taken off him. There were three physical contacts with him and Jane. Firstly, there was the pretty girl incident. There was also the earlier Mickey Mouse hug and then the Donald Duck hug, but he thinks that the costumed people were part of Hamleys, so it was unlikely to be the either of them that took the wallet. These three incidents happened over a hundred meters or so. Perhaps this is the pickpocketing area of London, Tom muses.

Tom and Jane get up and finish their day by going to a London Pub. Tom isn't worried about what happened now as he thinks there are more important things in life to worry about. He is still angry though and things like this grate Tom. He has an idea. He is here for two days. Today is with Jane so they can both catch up and be a tourist for the day, and tomorrow he had planned to walk the northern end of London as he loves the architecture there. He changes his mind now. Instead, tomorrow he will retrace the steps of today and keep an eye out for the pretty girl, Mickey Mouse and Donald Duck and see if he can spot one of them committing a crime. If he does see a steal he will know who took his wallet and he will challenge them. Tom won't be distracted by a pretty girl again, he thinks.

Tom and Jane say their goodbyes in the pub after a great day out together. Jane goes back to her east London flat to be with her flatmate and Tom goes to his hotel that he has booked for the night.

The following morning Tom plans out his day. He has got hold of a dummy iPhone case and has put it in his rear trouser pocket with a small, powerful mousetrap. He has loosened the pocket so that the dummy iPhone case is peeking out which will entice a pick-pocketer. Once the nasty trap is triggered the culprits fingers will bleed profusely from the thin, nasty wire. It is a little gruesome but Tom wants revenge.

Tom also wears an anorak, cap and sunglasses so that no-one recognises him from yesterday. He will start his search two hundred meters north of Hamleys and slowly make his way down the street, and this time he will people-watch.

As he approaches the Hamleys store he sees Mickey Mouse, who doesn't seem suspicious. He gets a bear hug again, but the trap isn't triggered so he carries on. He then goes past the chestnut stall and nods to the man. Again, all seems well.

The further down the street he sees Donald Duck. Just like yesterday Donald is not with the usual Hamleys costumed staff, but appears alone. As before, Donald Duck bear hugs him and this time Tom stumbles, and as that happens, a girl screams from behind Tom as the mousetrap has been triggered while his dummy iPhone is being taken. Tom recovers awkwardly from his stumble, but in the busy crowd he doesn't see the face of the girl who screamed. She must have run into the nearby alley. Tom is amazed at the speed at which the girl has scarpered.

Tom quickly darts down the quiet, narrow alley to chase after the girl who will be in trouble now that she has been rumbled. She will also be in pain now and Tom can see blood spots on the cobbled street floor. He is too slow to find her though. Tom continues down the long alley which leads back into Regent Street and the busy crowd. Damn, she is gone.

Tom gives up and seeks another coffee shop to drown his sorrows. He finds a quiet little shop where he can get a hot drink. While he has his coffee, he thinks back again. It was when Donald Duck hugged him that the girl pounced and took his dummy iPhone. This means that Donald Duck and the girl are working together. As he is thinking this, his eyes bulge as he has just spotted that pretty girl from yesterday through the coffee house glass window. She seems to be on her own, only a few yards away on the other side of the road eyeing up a potential steal, on the busy Oxford street pavement.

Tom gets up quickly, leaves the coffee shop, crosses the road and walks up to her through the bustling crowd. He grabs her collar roughly and spins her round, telling her that he will drag her to the police station. She shouts at him to let her go. It is then that Tom sees the scruffy man running away, where did he come from? Tom then notices the pretty girls hand.

Nothing. No blood at all and not even a scratch on either hand. He is surprised and has to let her go and she runs off. Tom continues his walk along the busy street and he soon sees in the distance the huge costume of Donald Duck again, so Tom runs fast to get to this costumed person.

Just as he reaches Donald Duck two undercover policemen seem to come out of nowhere and grab both Donald Duck and Donald's accomplice, who is hiding behind a bin. The accomplice is a girl in a hoody and as Tom gets to them, just two meters away, he realises that the accomplice is Jane, his sister.

He stares at Jane and then looks at her hand which is bleeding profusely.

Jane, now embarrassed is handcuffed alongside Donald Duck. The two of them have been pickpocketing together for weeks, and now they have been arrested. The head comes off Donald's costume and the person inside is revealed as Sue, Janes flatmate, who Tom recognises from Janes photo yesterday.

Toms London trip has come to a very sad end.

Short Story 11: Vices and Desires

The 1970's are difficult times, especially in the east end of London. Computers haven't arrived in people's homes yet and decimal currency has only just been adpoted. In this part of the world people struggle financially, but they make the best of what they have.

Dan and Daisy live in the far end of east London and they find life typically tough. They have been married for a few years now so both know each other's ways, some good and some not good at all. They have two teenagers. Harry is eighteen and takes after his dad in many ways, including playing rugby and supporting West Ham football club. Harriet is sixteen and keeps herself to herself. This is understandable as the two men of the household have a temper, so the wary Harriet opts for a quiet life by typically going upstairs to her room to avoid trouble. If things get too angry and loud at home she simply walks round to her friend's house in the next street and they visit the local pub.

Daisy is a cool, calm and collected mum, being the family organiser and a true matriarch. Dan is a plasterer by trade and for the last few years things have been going fairly well at work. This is the 1970's and many houses are being built in East London so he has plenty of work, which means at least the money is coming in. For some people payment of wages in 1970's is not through the bank but in the form of cash, to avoid tax, and Dan is paid cash every Wednesday night. He pays the bills and then puts the reminder of the cash in the pot on the living room mantlepiece, above the open fire. This way, if Daisy needs cash for food, kids clothes etc she can just use the money when it is needed. This worked well when they were first married but recently

Dan's vices have started to throttle the family. Apart from drinking in the local pub Dan has also been gambling. Gambling would be later known to be addictive but no one really knew at the time how destructive it could be in the 1970's. It would be gambling that would finally break this family up, but Dan doesn't realise it just now.

The gambling for Dan started a few years after they had been married. It was okay for a while as Dan earned well and although Daisy noticed that the amount of cash in the pot on the mantelpiece was getting lower by the day they never really ran out of money, so she didn't worry. However, Dan's silent addiction got worse and a few months ago the pot on the mantelpiece ran out of money completely, two days before Dan's payday.

Daisy had challenged Dan lightly a few times before but Dan had lied and said that he hadn't taken the money. Lying is a common factor in gamblers and it comes easy to them. Daisy knew he told lies to her as she had actually seen him take cash from the pot a few times when she looked through the open kitchen door. Dan would later deny it. He knew he was telling lies to his wife but couldn't help gambling, or telling untruths.

Dan and Daisy didn't talk about this to their children. Harry had heard mum and dads arguments about gambling but chose not to join in the accusations against dad. For years, and on average twice a week, the routine would be that first they would argue. Then, Dad would deny taking the cash, and then the following day he would apologise for lying and shouting, then complain to Daisy that he couldn't help gambling. Meanwhile Harry and Harriet would keep away from their parents and go upstairs. Harriet's reaction to the parental squabbles before she got a job was to go to do her homework upstairs or typically see her friend down the road and go to the pub.

Daisy tried not to argue too much at Dan. Besides, the two kids now had just started new jobs and were starting to earn their own money. Harry became a plasterer, like his dad, and worked for a builder in the next street. He was becoming even more like his dad now with his new job and interests. Harriet, being quiet and studious, worked as a secretary in an office a mere two-minute walk away, which was convenient. She earned just enough to get by and was getting more like her mum every day.

As the weeks went by Dan's work load became lighter and so payday resulted in less cash for the pot. Recently they had been breaking even, but only just. When their son Harry started working and began to add cash to the pot on the mantlepiece things became better, but after a while the cash would go somehow and they soon couldn't cover the bills. Daisy realised that over the years the cash was disappearing from the pot at the same rate as the number of nights that Dan came back late in the evenings.

One evening last week there was an almighty argument. Daisy challenged Dan yet again and the usual shouting routine followed, this time with more anger than usual as there was no money at all in the pot, and pay day for both Dan and Harry was not for another day. Dan shouted back at Daisy giving his standard denial that he didn't take the money, but Daisy knew what he was like and expected the usual apology the next day.

The next day came and instead of getting an apology from Dan Daisy saw him leave the house that evening in a strop. Harry had earlier put some cash in the pot during the afternoon and after they had all had tea the kids went upstairs to get out of the way while Dan left the house to see his mates in the pub. Daisy then went to take some money out of the pot to buy some food but the cash was gone; it was empty. She was internally fuming with Dan.

When the next day arrived, Daisy had calmed down but had started thinking about moving out and living with mum.

The next few days were better. On the Wednesday Dan had been paid so there was now some cash in the pot. So, while Harriet was quietly washing up Daisy gave an ultimatum to husband Dan while he and Harry were watching television in the living room, insight of the pot of cash on the mantlepiece.

She told Dan while he was watching television with Harry that she was going to see her mum for an hour and she expected the cash to still be there when she got back. She also asked them to be quiet as Harriet would be doing her secretarial coursework upstairs. Daisy hoped that Dan wouldn't mess up this time. She knows that Dan will have plenty of time to get to the pot if he really wants to as the living room is often unoccupied. It will be a test for him. She left the house to see her mum.

Dan and Harry looked at each other suspiciously while watching television alone in the room. When the programme finished Dan went to the kitchen for a drink. Harry went upstairs to listen to some music. This meant that Dan would soon return to the living room so would be on his own for a while and would therefore have potential access to the money pot, if his conscience didn't stop him. Ten minutes later Harry, upstairs, heard the front door slam as Dan left for the pub.

It is now an hour later and Daisy has returned to the house. Harry tells mum that dad had been on his own in the living room for a while and then left a while ago for the pub, while slamming the door. Daisy goes to the mantelpiece and opens the top of the pot and sees that there is nothing in it. Her blood boils while she refills it with four clean, crisp five-pound notes that her mum has just given her. She is angry with Dan and storms out of the house, leaving Harry and Harriet behind in the house. While she walks to the pub she constructs in her mind what she will say to her husband. She knows that his gambler friends tend to meet at the pub.

She arrives at the pub and it's no surprise that's he is there having a drink. However, she is surprised who he is with. He is talking to Bill, the town betting shop manager. Daisy is fuming now as she suspects the worst, but calms down when Bill tells her that he has refused money from Dan for two months now, as he knows Dan has a gambling problem. Daisy believes him as it is well known in town that Bill has done this before for other gamblers, so she makes her way back to the house. She now knows that Dan hasn't taken any money from the pot on the mantlepiece for two weeks, but someone has.

When she gets back to the house she goes to the living room and sees that Harry is sitting there watching television while eating the last mince pie from the fridge; and with a very guilty expression on his face.

She launches a verbal attack on him. Like-father-like-son, she tells him. Both are plasterers by trade and both support West Ham football club. They even share the same mannerisms. She now accuses him of being a gambler like his dad, taking the money for the last two months and letting dad take the blame. Then she storms out of the house.

Harry also leaves the house quickly to get away from mum. He can't stand her now.

Now that it is quiet in the house, the wary Harriet can come downstairs. She goes to the pot and takes out the four clean, crisp, five-pound notes out that grandma had given to Daisy earlier; just as Harriet has done for the last two months. She then takes her friend to the pub, knowing that her brother will get the blame.

Short Story 12: The Key To a Good Jury.

Karl has received a letter in this morning's post telling him that he has been called to attend jury service next month. This is annoying as he has just started his new career as a self-employed plumber and doesn't want anything to dampen his enthusiasm. However, this will be a jury service that will change his life.

Karl is now twenty-two and has just qualified from the local technical college and is raring to go to earn some money by setting up his own plumbing business. His dad works for a builder called Jan, a Dutchman who owns his own company. Karl has never met Jan but has seen him around the building site when he drops his dad off at work.

It was natural for Karl to go into the plumbing business as his dad was a handyman by trade, so he learned much from him. His hope is that if his dad's employer Jan, needs a plumber then he can earn some extra money by being on hand to help.

As well as passing his plumbing exams Karl has recently passed his driving test. As the family only have the one car dad has agreed that Karl should use it for his plumbing work, but he occasionally drops dad off at work, at whichever building site that might be.

Karl is a fit young lad, which helps in the plumbing trade as it is a very physical job. He doesn't have many other hobbies, so focuses on working out at the local gym every Tuesday night, which helps him to keep in trim. He enjoys pumping iron followed by a hot shower and perhaps a drink afterwards. Visits to the gym are usually on his own but occasionally dad joins him for some simple exercise. Karl doesn't know anyone else at the gym but sometimes sees his old school teacher there, as well as dad's boss, Jan.

It's a Monday morning now and Karl and his dad are in the car approaching dads work, at one of the building sites. While driving, Karl looks at the huge bunch of dad's keys dangling in the ignition and laughs. They contain about twenty keys, comprising both car and work keys, all in one huge bundle. There is even a massive garden gate key, and also a thick Chubb key which digs into his dads pocket every time he gets them out. Karl asks his dad why he needs so many keys, but dad responds by telling him to concentrate on his driving. As the car slows down at a set of traffic lights Karl talks to dad about Jan, the boss. There has been some gossip about both him and his associates being involved in a robbery, then hiding the cash in a garage lock up somewhere nearby. Dad ignores him.

The only set of garages Karl has seen in his young life are those he has seen on television programmes, and also those behind Gran's house. He remembers being a young lad kicking a ball against Grans garage with his friend, and he smirks as he also remembers losing his temper with his friend on one occasion, then kicking the garage door next to grans and leaving a nasty dent at the bottom. He had to apologise to Grans neighbour. Thinking of Gran reminds him that she will be going into a care home next month, once his parents have saved enough money to pay for the deposit.

Karl drops his dad off and attends the three plumbing jobs he has in his diary for today. They are all pretty straightforward and he gets home earlier than expected. He still lives with mum and dad in the family home, but not for long, he hopes. Mum and dad have been in trouble with the police before and are not a good influence on him, so he hopes to find a flat for himself soon. He will need a few thousand pounds for a down payment though.

While he has tea with mum she tries to quiz him about the upcoming jury service. However, Karl knows little of what Jury service is all about. He hopes it will be a quick and simple one, perhaps a minor theft. Then he can get back to earning some money to pay for the flat that he is keen to buy. After tea he leaves mum downstairs and goes upstairs to his room.

A few weeks later it is time for jury service and Karl gets to Reading court on time.

All the jurors get a briefing, which is very intense and Karl struggles to take it all in. The jury are soon shuffled into court and take their seats.

The accused is brought in and Karl takes a good look at him. They have been warned not to make judgements simply on appearances but Karl can't help getting a sense of what this man is like. He stares at the man and thinks that he has seen him before, but is not sure where. There is no time to think though as the session starts and the Judge makes the introductions.

As the day progresses Karl gets bored very easily with the tedium of court. He still can't help but think that he has seen the accused before. This man reminds him of someone but he does not know who it is. It is only when he hears the accused's name, Henk de Venn that he realises that the accused is Dutch and then he makes the connection that he looks very much like his dad's boss, Jan. It isn't actually Jan himself, but looks like him and Karl is convinced that he must be the brother of Jan, as his mannerisms and features are so similar. Karl doesn't know the surname of Jan but he does look like him and when the accused confirms his address Karl realises that this man lives in the same town as Jan. Karl is now convinced that he is on the jury of the brother of his dad's boss.

The accused is charged with stealing a hundred thousand pounds from a bank and then hiding it in a garage lock up somewhere. This is similar to the gossip that Karl spoke to his dad about. The police don't know where the lock up is but they have fingerprint evidence to show that that this man took the money. To Karl, this is a trial that will be a formality and the accused will be found guilty in a day or two. However, nobody from the public has come forward with any help. Even the ten-thousand-pound reward offered by the police for information has not yielded results. The police have searched through the Dutchman's phone texts and the only information the court have as to the whereabouts of the money is a text from the accused, to an unknown phone, that the garage lockup has two padlocks, with two separate keys. They have a picture of the two keys, which they also found on his smartphone. It is not a very good picture but clear enough for Karl to see, when it is shown to the jury.

The accused also smugly states that he is the only one who knows where the money has been stashed, so it seems that the man in the dock is the only one who knows where both the two keys to the lockup and the money are.

Throughout the course of the trial the prosecution interrogates the Dutchman as to the whereabouts of the keys. While Karl sits there the Jury listens to the Dutchman's reply, but he gives nothing away. The picture shows that one key is a thick Chubb key and the other is a tiny Yale key.

Then Karl starts to link things together. He also has a tiny Yale key, for his gym locker, which looks just like the one in the court photo. Its padlock also looks like the type he uses at the gym, and he knows that the accused's brother Jan goes to his gym, so could it be that the accused goes there also? Karl reflects on this and now thinks that the Yale key must be from the gym. Henk is probably keeping it safe in Jan's locker there. It wouldn't be hard for Karl to check this out and go to the gym, then work out which locker to pick. After all the lockers are not very secure there.

Then he thinks about the other key that court has talked about. He realises that he has also seen a thick Chubb key before, similar to the one in the court photo. There is a Chubb key on dad's works keyring, and his dad has said he doesn't know what it's for, as it's amongst all the other work keys. Perhaps the accused's brother, Jan, has hidden this

Chubb key alongside dad's work keys, which would be a clever place to hide it.

Karl doesn't believe that all this information he is learning about today is a coincidence as there are too many pieces of the jigsaw now that fit together. He is convinced that he can get hold of the keys if he wants to get the money, but where actually is the money?

As the trial progresses, the prosecution eventually talks about the money. The accused hasn't told anyone where it is hidden, but in the police interview notes, which the Jury pre-read, it mentioned a rusty lock-up garage. There is a photo of the garage door and Karl realises now that it is not just rusty, but also has a dent at the bottom, exactly like Grans neighbours garage door does. Karl is sure now that this stolen money is the money that dad had been talking about recently. He is also sure that other than the accused, he is now the only one in court who knows all three pieces of information that the court does not know, which are the whereabouts of the two keys and the money.

Karl smiles to himself. The accused is sitting there smugly thinking that he is the only one who knows all this information. Not anymore.

The first thoughts come together for Karl to get hold of a huge amount of money.

After day one at court Karl returns home and goes straight to the pub. He needs thinking time. He buys himself a couple of pints and constructs a money-making plan. Two pints turn into many pints after his best friend at school, and now gym partner, Sam joins him. Karl is now tells his court story to Sam. He then walks back home where mum and dad are not impressed by his alcoholic state. They also hear the story from court.

Unfortunately for Karl, after his high excitement of being at court, he has now told three other people what he knows regarding the keys and the money.

The next day Karl has calmed down. On his way to court he is musing over whether he could get hold of the two keys and get to the garage lock-up without anyone knowing.

Then, he can get access to some serious money. He gets to court for the next day's session and is told that he is only needed for another two days. He suspects that this is because they think that the case will wrap up soon and the Dutchman will be convicted.

That night Karl goes to the gym and it's not long before he finds Henk's hidden Yale key.

He now has an exact plan for how to get some serious money and makes a phone call, then goes home and rummages around his dad's keys and finds what he needs. He now has the Chubb key and so now has both keys that are needed for the job.

Karl then gets ready to use his dad's car. He will meet his phone contact near Grans garage lockup tonight, and begins to daydream of easy money. At 5pm on this wet, dark Tuesday night he drives to the set of garages where Grans rusty garage is located.

When he gets there, he parks a little further up the road so that he doesn't look suspicious and waits in the car for his phone contact to arrive. He looks at the dent at the bottom of the rusty door next door to grans garage and imagines what is behind it.

Soon, a car approaches, drives past him and stops at the garages, but Karl is shocked. The driver isn't the person he rang. Instead it's his dad in a car that he has rented for some reason.

He watches his dad get out of the car in the dark, take out a crowbar from the boot, and then sizes up the garage next door to grans that Karl has told him contains the cash. His dad has worked it out and now he wants some cash too.

Then Karl hears another car coming, this time it is a marked police car. Karl winds down his window and shouts to his dad that the police are coming.

His dad looks up. He is shocked as he didn't expect his son to be there at all in the dark, but he sees the police car and shoots off quickly in his rented car.

The police car slows down, parks near Grans garage and out steps a policeman.

Karl gets out of his car to meet the policeman, who is the person that he had phoned earlier. He gives the policeman the two keys that he got hold of earlier in the day and shows him the garage next door to grans. The policeman opens the garage and finds the stash of money.

The policeman smiles and comments that Karl does indeed deserve the ten-thousand-pound reward that was available.

Karl smiles back. No need to be greedy, he thinks. He might as well have a legal ten-thousand-pound Police reward, rather than a stolen one hundred thousand pounds, where he might get found out.

That's the down payment for the flat sorted.

Gran can get into that care home as well.

Karl smiles again.

Short Story 13: The Perfect Escape.

So, we now come to the last three stories. These were the three that Uncle Chris had chosen to read to Sandy. It was another cold winter's night high up in the snowy Welsh mountains. Uncle Chris, sitting in front of his roaring log fire, was enjoying its warmth in his luxury log cabin, which was situated halfway up one of the highest mountains in Wales. He was reminiscing to Sandy about past stories that he always enjoyed sharing. He loved to tell stories to her, all of which had a little twist that always fooled her.

Uncle Chris was an ageing World War II war veteran, who had spent much time in occupied France during the combat. He was enjoying a post meal shot of rum, his favourite tipple, in front of the roaring fire. Sandy, being only a youngster preferred mango juice. Uncle Chris enjoyed telling her stories including those from the war, and Sandy loved to hear them, trying to work out if they were real or fictional.

Uncle Chris had a story about a particular secret prisoner of war camp in France close to the German border, which the Germans built when they had occupied France in the second world war. The camp had housed many war prisoners who were either English, French or Polish. Prisoners of the camp were continually looking for ways to escape and Uncle Chris decided it was time to tell Sandy his secret story of one incident when some of the prisoners escaped.

Uncle Chris began. "Well, Sandy, I'll tell you a true story about an escape that no one knows about, as it's classified and only the authorities know about it."

"Wow," said Sandy, "tell me more." Uncle Chris sometimes invented stories to catch young Sandy out but as this story was about the war then Sandy thought that it might be true.

Uncle Chris took a sip of rum, leant back in his armchair and boomed, "It was a well-planned escape Sandy. I'll give you the facts and let's see if you can work out how it was done."

"You are too young to know what a prisoner of war camp looks like, or a POW camp as the soldiers called it, but imagine about ten large wooden huts, with a total of three hundred prisoners held in them, in a big camp. Over the months and years of the war many attempts were made by the three hundred POWs to escape and attempt to reach England. They tried various ways to escape, some attempts included using clever disguises. Other methods involved digging tunnels under dormitory floorboards, which could hold and hide a few men. The tunnels extended under the perimeter fence so that they could escape. They even tried to make an aeroplane once! However, even though they had all these escape ideas ready to go without the Germans knowing, they couldn't work out the final details of how to get out. The problem was that getting a reasonable number of people out, say ten rather than just one, meant that many sets of civilian clothes would be needed, and when they got out how would they get all the escapees through the countryside quickly and back to England with all the German soldiers chasing them? So, you can imagine that a lot of work was done to no avail. Also, the German solders kept an eye on the prisoner numbers by conducting roll calls, which were done twice a day to count the three hundred POWs."

Uncle Chris supped his rum again. "Then, a bright spark prisoner came up with a clever idea, a way to get ten people out of the French POW camp without the Germans working out what was going on. He used the previous knowledge and resources from the past escape attempts and then created a new plan for people to escape. The POW escape team managed to get word to the English on how the escape would work. This was done well before the escape, using Morse code with help from the French Resistance in the small town nearby. The Resistance would also send written messages back to the POWs in camp. These would be delivered by the town's driver of the weekly food truck for the camp."

Uncle Chris continued, "The big escape had to happen late on a Friday as the German soldiers had some down time then. They would be drinking so they wouldn't be as attentive as usual. It also had to be a damp night, so it was decided that it would be Friday 3rd November for the night of the big escape, when the Germans would be alerted to ten POWs missing. They would then begin the search".

"Sure enough, at the 6pm roll call on this day the Germans had only two hundred and ninety of the three hundred POWs attend the roll call, and they realised that ten POWs were missing. They quickly started a search of the camp. This was soon aborted when one of the soldiers found a hole in the wire fence, big enough for people to squeeze through, with many different footprints in the wet mud and freshly laid snow, leading to the adjacent forest. All the soldiers quickly assembled near the hole in the fence. They got an armed search party together, including dogs, and began the search in the forest for the missing ten POWs, hoping to catch them before they got to the town, where they could hide."

Sandy, only a youngster herself, looked outside of the window of their log cabin. She saw the snow and asked, "Was the snow as bad there as it is here?"

"Oh yes," said Uncle Chris, "and it was important that the escape was done at this time of year. The soldiers, with their dogs, followed the footprints and searched the forest. They soon came to an area of ground where numerous footprints in the snow were accompanied by ten sets of prisoner clothes, discarded on the ground. The soldiers looked at the clothes and concluded that the ten escapees had changed out of their camp prisoner clothes into some civilian clothes that they had made and brought with them. The search then continued in the forest for the ten escapees in civilian clothes".

"I bet they all got to England then Uncle Chris?" said Sandy.

"No Sandy, the Germans very quickly found one of the POWs. His name was Guy Foster. They thought this to be a rather useless escape attempt as he had neither a passport nor money to get to another country, probably thinking that the French Resistance in the local small town would help. Anyway, he was picked up in town close to the baker's shop and the Post Office, and he was instantly shot by one of the soldiers. His clothes were searched, but all they found on him were some minor coins and a small notepad with a pencil. The notepad had one page ripped out, but the indent on the next page clearly showed his name written, "Guy F". This seemed odd as there were no other words in the sentence. They brought his body back to camp quickly as the French Resistance were known to have a presence in town. They didn't find the other nine POWs".

"Over the next twenty-four hours none of the other nine escapees were found and the Germans had no idea where they were nor how they had evaded them. Two days later, on the 5th November, the English papers were rejoicing that nine POWs had returned to England. The German soldiers couldn't believe that their dogs couldn't find the nine English POWs in the forest, or on the long trip to the town."

Uncle Chris continued. "So, Sandy, you can imagine how upset the Germans were. The hole in the perimeter fence was mended and they made sure that the remaining POWs suffered over the next few days. The Camp Commander also wanted to know why his soldiers had only found one of the POWs who had escaped and, having done that, why they were not able to trace any of the other nine, either in the forest or in the town. He was convinced that they could not have all got through the forest untraced. Yet, the English papers told him that they had returned home. The Commander asked for increased security, and even more roll calls per day were performed by the Germans to make that sure there were no more escapes."

"This seemed to work because over the few weeks until Christmas, every roll call had the correct two hundred and ninety POWs attending, so the Germans were confident of no more escapees. The only unusual event was a couple of days after Guy Foster was captured, when one of the new German soldiers in town noticed some 'locals' who he hadn't seen before. He wasn't sure if it was because he was new to the area so as a precaution he called the camp to see if anyone had escaped from camp, but an immediate roll call showed two hundred and ninety inmates so the Germans were not concerned. However, they still couldn't work out how the original nine POWs got to England without being noticed."

"So, Sandy," enquired Uncle Chris "Have you managed to work out how the other nine prisoners got to England yet?"

"No," replied Sandy, "I don't know how they did it. How did they escape from the German soldiers and their dogs in the forest?"

"Well" explained Uncle Chris, "in camp, the POWs had plenty of ideas on how to escape but, even if they got out they knew it was a long way to the French resistance in town through the forest. They also knew that they would get caught as soon as the Germans heard of the escape, so they had to find a way where they would not think anyone had escaped. So a plan was hatched where there was not one but two escape attempts. One where only one POW escaped and another a few days later when nine POWs would escape".

Uncle Chris continued, "In the first escape on 3rd November only one POW actually escaped and that was Guy Foster. The Germans were made to think that ten had escaped as the roll call showed two hundred and ninety POWs instead of three hundred. That's because nine POWs were hidden under the floor boards of the prisoner huts, in the old unused escape tunnels, while just one escaped. The nine were hidden by the POWs during all roll calls over the next few days to fool the Germans into thinking that they had escaped also.

So, the Germans were now looking in the forest for ten escaped POWs, nine of which were hiding under the floorboards while Guy Foster himself had escaped through the wire fencing."

"After the Germans saw the English newspapers, they had thought that the nine POWs had got to England. Things got back to normal in the POW camp soon after. The nine POWs who were hiding under the floor boards would then a few days later complete the second escape by leaving through one of the old escape tunnels. The Germans would not know they had escaped as the roll call numbers would still be at two hundred and ninety (and also, they had thought that they had escaped earlier so they wouldn't be looking for them). As long as the Germans didn't find the tunnel under the dormitory floorboards then they wouldn't know a second escape had taken place."

After another sip of his drink Uncle Chris said "So, for the first escape, to make the Germans think that ten had escaped instead of just one, Guy Foster the lone escapee, would take a few pairs of boots and clothes to dump as soon as he got to the forest, for the Germans to find. He had run as fast as he could to get to the Post Office. The staff had previously been alerted to the planned escape days earlier by the camp food truck driver who had got word of this from the POWs".

"The food truck driver was a regular visitor and frequently passed on messages to and from the camp. When he got to the post office Guy had passed on the written message from his notebook to the Post office. The message was to be Morse coded to England by the French resistance, and it was simply "Guy F" which the English knew stood for Guy Fawkes and it signalled to them that November 5th was therefore the day that they needed to put in the papers the false information that nine POWs had arrived in England. You see Sandy, November 5th is celebrated as

Bonfire Night in England, where Guy Fawkes is remembered, and all the English people know that. Of course, the nine POWs hadn't arrived in England but the Germans needed to be convinced that they had succeeded so that they would stop looking for them. The remaining nine POWs hiding in the tunnel simply needed to wait until things had quietened down in camp and then use the tunnel (already made for previous attempts) for the second escape. When they did escape the Germans would not realise they had gone, as the roll call still announced two hundred and ninety POWs."

"But why was a snowy day needed Uncle Chris?" asked Sandy.

"Sandy, the weather was important to lay down the misdirections such as the snow footprints from the sets of shoes that Guy took with him, to suggest to the Germans that ten people had escaped."

Uncle Chris continued. "Also, the timing of the first escape had to be a few days before the 5th November, Bonfire night. This was so that the Guy Fawkes message would confirm to the British papers that Nov 5th was the day they should announce the false statement for the arrival of the nine POWs in the newspapers. Of course, it meant one POW would actually anticipate to be captured, as his role was to trigger the false Morse code message to the papers. He had hoped to be returned to his buddies, but he was shot by the soldiers instead. His nine buddies escaped though."

"And that" said Uncle Chris "was how the nine POWs escaped'.

"But Uncle Chris" said Sandy "you said this was a true story, but how did you hear about it and get all this detail if, as you say, no-one knew about it other than the authorities. You weren't even a POW yourself?"

"I wasn't a POW" replied Uncle Chris, "but I was an excellent POW camp food truck driver! Vive la France Sandy."

With that Uncle Chris had another shot of rum.

Short Story 14: To Do or Not To Do.

It was almost midnight and it had started to freeze in the darkness of the Welsh mountains. In their log cabin Uncle Chris and Sandy were continuing to warm themselves by the flickering flames in the snug fireplace. Uncle Chris was keeping fuelled with alcohol from his umpteenth rum of the evening. Sandy watched Uncle Chris sup his rum and was keen for yet another story while she gulped her Mango juice.

Uncle Chris soon spoke from his armchair. "Sandy, I have a story for you, it's about the first time that my best friend secured a job in England and yes, it's another true story!"
Sandy's attention was grabbed now as Uncle Chriss' stories were usually fictional.

Uncle Chris leaned back in his armchair and the story started.

"My friend was confronted with a minor crime that happened a long time ago at a company in southern England, in the summer of 1984. This research site was a lovely converted old mansion house which held a combination of offices and laboratories inside it. In the building there were about sixty employees, most of whom were under thirty years of age. Many were fresh from college, finding their way in industry for the first time and meeting new friends of their own age, both at work and in their social life. Some worked in the offices, others in the laboratories. The work was good fun and most of the staff got on well as the social life was plentiful and the area was nice to live in. Mind you, it was very expensive being near London."

Uncle Chris continued "The work force consisted of both young and experienced scientists, managers, secretaries (they were called that in those days), financial staff and of course an I.T. man who looked after the computers, which were a new thing in the 1980's. This was an English research building reporting to the company headquarters site based on the other side of the world, meaning that many phone calls were made across the world every day from this site."

"Does anybody die in this story Uncle Chris?" asked Sandy

Uncle Chris's eyes went north and replied. "No, but a strange crime was committed. Now, Sandy, this might sound ancient to you but this happened in May 1989 so emails, texts, and mobile phones weren't available and communicating with the outside world was all about using the telephone. So, everybody had an individual desk phone, with their own extension number".

Sandy glanced at his mobile phone. Uncle Chris is very old and can be really old fashioned sometimes, she thought.

Uncle Chris ignored Sandy's smile. "The problem started at the end of May. Most people behaved themselves but one person took liberties and decided to make personal telephone calls to Taiwan on a regular basis, which was extremely expensive for the company and also broke work rules. Presumably the calls were to a friend or family, no-one knew.

The culprit managed to keep it secret for a while but everyone soon knew that someone was making inappropriate phone calls, which was a sackable offence."

"The company obviously wanted to find out who was making these calls. Sandy, why don't you be a little detective? I'll give you all the facts you need and you can work out how the culprit was identified."

"Okay Uncle Chris, I'll give it a go" Sandy replied and she listened intently, waiting for the clues.

Uncle Chris continued. "The I.T. manager offered to investigate and identify the person responsible. He had experienced a similar event in a previous job and he had found the culprit himself, so the building manager asked him to find the person making these calls. The I.T. man realised that whoever was making the calls was sneaky, using other people's office or lab phone instead of their own. Everyone had an individual phone on their desk so there were plenty around for the culprit to choose from. This person made the calls over the summer at different times of the day so it was hard to catch him or her out. Calls were made a few times a week and on separate days. The I.T. man could get a print out of all the calls made by everyone at the end of each day, so the company could track when these calls were made and on which phone. It was always to the same number in Taiwan. The I.T. man also had access to details of each employee's personal file such as bank records, previous jobs, number of holidays taken etc".

"So" continued Uncle Chris. "How do you catch someone making a phone call to somewhere he or she shouldn't do during the day, when technology is limited and everyone is working hard making legitimate phone calls? The telephone printout would give the I.T. man the days output at the end of the day, in terms of what telephone numbers were being called, from which phone, and when. However, the limited I.T. technology in those days meant that you only got that information at the end of the day and you couldn't be notified when anyone was actually making a call. So, the villain couldn't be caught in the act."

Sandy jumped in. "You can't sit next to everyone at work and watch what they are doing."

"Exactly." Uncle Chris agreed. "So the I.T. man had a difficult job to track down the culprit and find out when these calls were being made. After all, he had his daily job to do as well. Life was easy for the culprit because any of the staff could be at meetings, lunch, coffee breaks or even off sick, so their phones could be available for him or her to make a quick call when a phone was vacant".

Uncle Chris continued. "The company had a few guesses as to who the culprit was. Recently four students had been recruited to help in the laboratory, so they were suspects as these calls started only weeks after they had begun working. They also had suspicions for a few of the other workers for various reasons. In all, about twelve people were on their suspect list, and they were all male."

Sandy jumped in. "All male? Is that because girls never do anything wrong? That's what mum says."

"A coincidence I'm sure" replied Uncle Chris a bit grumpily. "For one reason or another the managers couldn't work out who was making the rogue calls, but finally in September the I.T. man said that he had identified the culprit and the managers met to look at his evidence."

Uncle Chris continued. "The next day one of the male students was summoned to the company managers office where he was challenged. He admitted making the calls and was dismissed.

So, Sandy, you have all the information now. Can you work out how the company found out who was doing it?" asked Uncle Chris.

"I am not sure, it could have been anyone." said Sandy.

"Well, I've given you all the facts, but I'll give you a clue. You can work it out by the Sherlock Holmes principal which is?"

Sandy thought she knew this. "Once you have discounted the impossible then whatever remains must be the truth, or something like that, I can't remember it well, but I still don't know how it was done. How did the I.T. man work it out Uncle Chris?"

Uncle Chris smiled as he had fooled Sandy again with one of his stories.

"It was all by process of elimination really, Sherlock's way of discounting the impossible. The culprit wouldn't have wanted to use his own phone, so he used other people's phones. That means there's a good chance that he wasn't the owner of those phones. That helped to narrow down the field, don't forget, he was making many phone calls per week. The I.T. man had each employee's personal records and also the print out of daily telephone records. That was all he needed, he analysed the information and then he could discount the impossible, as Sherlock would".

Sandy still looked confused, so Uncle Chris continued. "Eleven people on the suspect list were each eliminated because they were on holiday or were ill on at least one of the days when a call to Taiwan was made. That left one person, this student, as the only possibility, and then he made his biggest mistake. It was in something that he didn't do, not that he did do. The young man was found out because there was only one person in August who had a two-week holiday which matched the time that there were no calls made at all, and that was him. He can't make calls from a work phone if he isn't there".

Sandy suddenly got it and smiled.

Uncle Chris ended with "It's not what you do that catches you out Sandy, sometimes it's what you don't do, and in this case the student didn't use the phone for two weeks."

With that, Uncle Chris smiled, leant back, and had another rum.

Short Story 15: Life's a Breeze.

The next day Sandy had a friend come to visit him at the log cabin. Dawn was Sandy's age and lived near her back home. They were good friends and both enjoyed sledging with Uncle Chris all day in the fresh, white snow of the mountains. They then played snow games until they needed a break from the cold.

Dawn's family had made their wealth from the advertising industry. She was fit and strong and loved the outdoors, so both youngsters had much in common. In the evening, after tea, they looked out of the log cabin window to see that it was getting dark quickly. They loved the luxury log cabin, it was so cosy and had everything they needed.

While having his usual shot of evening rum Uncle Chris re-lit the fire and it was just about flickering with life now. The youngsters were settling down on the soft settee while supping on some mango juice. Dawn had heard about Uncle Chriss legendary fictional stories, especially the ones with a little twist to fool you. However, Uncle Chris's furrowed brow suggested that this one may be true, and serious.

Uncle Chris started. "This story is about Jonathan Smythe and how he coped with terrible adversity and turned it into something positive. He is a very interesting character and you would both do well to learn from his experiences. He was born in the stockbroker town of Guildford, into a wealthy family with, as the phrase goes, a silver spoon in his mouth. His father, Victor Smythe, owned three private schools in Guildford and was the President of the Guildford Bowls club. Victor very much enjoyed his mansion estate home and also the large lake in the garden containing his prize Koi carp. He was a keen tennis player and had his own court at the rear of their huge garden.

Jonathan's mother Angela also played tennis. She spent most of her time bringing up Jonathan, which included teaching him the piano and the flute. She was also excellent at golf and was captain of the local golf club."

Uncle Chris continued. "Jonathan himself inherited his parent's talents and was by far the most gifted pupil in the south of England. He was soon earning money as a teenager teaching younger children the piano. Life was good for him. He was a tall, well-spoken young man with slightly curly hair, which was cut short. He looked a bit geeky, which matched his musical talents and was also brilliant at all sports, with the kind of natural talent most of us are jealous of."

"Not like me then" said Sandy. "He sounds more like you Dawn as you love your football and croquet."

"I'm more worried about what your Uncle Chris has got to say next" said Dawn, looking at Uncle Chris's rum.

Uncle Chris continued. "Everything fell into place for Jonathan Smythe in his early years. He succeeded in primary school and secondary school, had first team appearances in all the sports he played. He even had a charming girlfriend. All without trying. Money was no barrier due to the wealth and success of his parents, whatever he needed he got.

The easy life continued when he went to Oxford University to read Classics. He specialised in Greek History, got a first degree and thoroughly enjoyed Oxford life, both academically and socially. He gave piano recitals at many of the colleges and got an Oxford Blue for football. Life continued to be good. Jonathan even bought his own flat."

"Then his life changed dramatically and he realised that things wouldn't come as easily in life in the future. He was a passenger in a friend's car and the accident on an Oxford country road was brutal and meant his left leg had to be amputated."

Sandy and Dawn's faces turned white, reflecting the coloured flames of the fire.

Uncle Chris continued as the youngsters listened in. "Everything changed, he was now disabled and had to walk with crutches. Contact with his friends was reduced. For some reason they weren't available and girls weren't so keen to meet up with him. Having only one leg and using crutches meant he also struggled with his love of sports. After the initial shock since the accident, he did manage to play football in a disabilities team, but only with the use of a crutch, and with peers of the same ilk who also found it frustrating."

"It took a while to come to terms with only having one leg. He considered a prosthetic but instead continued with the crutches. He struggled with life and had bouts of depression and drugs. I am sad to say the drugs were not of the medicinal kind."

Sandy and Dawn looked at each other while Uncle Chris continued.

"His parents didn't help as they didn't realise that he wasn't coping well in his flat. Leaving university life meant that Jonathan needed a job. He found employment with an industrial firm as a Marketing Manager and this took his mind off his sadness. He was of course brilliant at the job and did well, but again struggled to get around with one leg. Carrying both a laptop and coffee around offices with crutches isn't easy.

With a determined effort he started to gain confidence and got back on the road again. Although this time he had to fight for everything".

"Then a chance meeting with a friend's friend in a pub changed his life. He was introducing himself to the new acquaintance who asked him about the car crash. When Jonathon had finished his reply, the chap gave him some advice about being disabled, then made the flippant comment that Jonathan would soon pull himself together. Jonathan asked how he could possibly know what it was like to be disabled. Then the chap tapped at his own leg with the knuckles on his hand. There was a wooden sound as the man had a prosthetic leg. Jonathan couldn't tell he was disabled by the way he walked so was shocked to see that he had a wooden leg. It did make Jonathan think again about prosthetics, but he still didn't want an artificial leg because he felt people should see what life was like for him. However, this chap gave him an idea".

Uncle Chris could see that the two of them were wondering where this story was going. They would get a surprise soon, he reckoned.

"As Jonathan had wealthy parents and he was now also disabled, he had the bright idea of putting both to good use.

He set up a number of initiatives which included buying a small building in town and setting it up with a variety of disability facilities and he allowed people to come and use these sports and leisure facilities. He also provided laptops with physical aids for the disabled, so they could come in and use them when needed. Many under privileged disabled people came to use the facilities, for free. He became a bit of a local star. Jonathan linked up with the local council and really pioneered the towns disability initiative."

Sandy kept listening. "What a great idea, especially as his family had the money to help". She was captivated. Dawn was even more focused on Uncle Chris's story, she could tell something was up Uncle Chris's sleeve. Uncle Chris looked at the youngsters and smiled, wondering if they had guessed the twist to his story.

He continued. "Then one day Jonathan was asked to give a lecture at a seminar in Romania, on working in industry with a disability. The Romanians were not as well set up as the English regarding the public's perception of disability but were starting to improve and needed examples where there had been successes in other countries. Jonathan was proud to be asked to talk to them. The flight to the airport in Romania wasn't too bad although the airline wasn't equipped very well for anyone other than business people. Once off the plane he made the long, slow and painful walk towards customs and saw two huge queues to get through.

This would be hard work with only one leg. He knew there were some countries who were well equipped for disabled people and some that were even prejudiced against disability. Jonathan wasn't sure how the Romanians were set up. He watched carefully as the staff marshalled people, around. He was then told abruptly by security to go into a particular queue. Jonathan told him that he wasn't impressed by the man's manner, but he simply looked back at Jonathan, unimpressed with his pompous English reply. Jonathan was also unimpressed by the Romanians as he noticed that there were some disabled people in this particular queue. Here, each person seemed to spend more time being interviewed at customs than the other queue, who all seemed to be able well-dressed business men. Perhaps he should mention this in his presentation, as well as a lack of airport disabled facilities".

"As he slowly made it to the front of the customs queue he became increasing angry at everyone's attitude and reaction to him. He became self-conscious about his missing leg and while he was waiting in the queue he thought about how he had got this far. Wealthy Surrey parents, golf club, bowls club, mansion house, university, accident, disability, grind, job, and now telling the Romanians about disability."

Uncle Chris paused, supped his rum, looked at both youngsters and continued.

"At the front of the queue the customs officer looked at Jonathan, asked him many personal questions, and then further questions about where he was going. Jonathan thought that the people in the other queue didn't get this level of attention. He finally got through after a lengthy interrogation.

Jonathan did give his disability lecture at the conference later in the day, but he was more than happy to return home to England as soon as possible.

When he got back to his comfortable flat Jonathan sat in his armchair with a coffee and reflected on how he had come though the disappointments of his disability and turned it into something positive, very positive. Hopefully his advice will be soon be taken up by the Romanian authorities."

Uncle Chris looked at the youngsters in front of the roaring fire and lowered his tone so that his voice sounded mysterious.

"Sandy and Dawn, you know what? Even today, Jonathan doesn't know if he was stopped at customs for so long just because he was disabled. It occurred to him that it might also have been because he was black."

There was a silence in the log cabin.

Sandy now realised she had been fooled by another of Uncle Chris's stories.

Dawn then smiled as she had had the same thought.

Sandy stared at Dawn and then at Uncle Chris, thoughts whirring through her mind. She gradually smiled and said to Uncle Chris.

"I presumed he was a white man, but he was black…as are the three of us." And all three of them smiled.

Uncle Chris leant back in his chair, ran his hand through his now grey, receding curly Afro hair. He then smiled at the girls and supped another Caribbean rum, which he had bought last year from his native home in Antigua.

The End

Acknowledgements

My thanks go to Chris for all his help, Caroline for her advice and the fabulously gorgeous Kate of course.

If you enjoyed this book then try the first book in the series: *Uncle Chris's Collection of Crafty Short Stories*.

Will the twist meister be back again……?
Oh yes indeed. Look for *Uncle Chris's **Third** Collection of Crafty Short Stories* in the summer of 2025.

Money raised will contribute to
"worldvision.org.uk/support"
who support vulnerable children worldwide.

www.ingramcontent.com/pod-product-compliance
Ingram Content Group UK Ltd.
Pitfield, Milton Keynes, MK11 3LW, UK
UKHW040437280225
455666UK00003B/132

9 781835 635643